MALVA

MALVA

Hagar Peeters

translated by Vivien D. Glass

DoppelHouse Press | Los Angeles

Malva
By Hagar Peeters
Copyright: © 2015 Hagar Peeters. Originally published by De Bezige Bij, Amsterdam

Translated from the Dutch by Vivien D. Glass
Copyright © 2018 Vivien D. Glass

DoppelHouse Press gratefully acknowledges the support of the Dutch Foundation
for Literature.

ederlands
letterenfonds
dutch foundation
for literature

Cover design: Kourosh Beigpour
Typesetting: Jody Zellen

Publisher's Cataloging-in-Publication data
Names: Peeters, Hagar, 1972- author. | Glass, Vivien D., translator.
Title: Malva / by Hagar Peeters ; translated by Vivien D. Glass.
Description: Los Angeles, CA: DoppelHouse Press, 2018.
Identifiers: ISBN 9780999754405 (Hardcover) | 9780999754429 (pbk.) |
9780999754498 (ebook) | LCCN 2018937176
Subjects: LCSH Reyes, Malva Marina, 1934-1943--Fiction. | Neruda, Pablo,
1904-1973--Family--Fiction. | Fathers and daughters--Fiction. | Family--Fiction.
| Neruda, Pablo, 1904-1973--Relations with women--Fiction. | Hagenaar, Maria
Antonia--Fiction. | Poets, Chilean--Fiction. | Chile--History--20th century--Fiction.
| BISAC FICTION / Historical. | FICTION / Literary. | FICTION / Magical Realism |
FICTION / Women authors.
Classification: LCC PT5881.26 .E49 .M35 2018 | LCC 839.3--dc23

PRINTED IN THE UNITED STATES

DoppelHouse Press
Los Angeles, California

GODSAKE THAT FATHER OF MINE was always cock
of the walk when it came to social injustice.
He was a fellow traveler, mover
on the waves of history, describing them
with a steady hand, bullet-free and steadfastly
venturing far into distant misty cities,
further than the shirt and the skirt
my mother hitched up
to give birth to me.

Dammit my father whom I was so proud of
I wanted to follow him,
a little kiddie companion
even on his knee I traveled upsy-daisy
on a camel through the desert with the caravan
far away from her who for years to come
lay moaning in her bedroom
letting in neither sleep nor daylight,
no outside air, no foreign land
and no fatherly face to make her wilt further
than my birth

but my father, ay ay compañero, was in Chile,
Nicaragua, on a steam liner crossing the ocean,
in a Bolivian clink with beard, knife and hat
thinking the world too small for him
while she raised a whole new life on her own.

My footprints melt in snow.
They take the shape of an accidental animal
then suddenly vanish halfway.

ONE

MY NAME IS MALVA MARINA Trinidad del Carmen Reyes, Malvie to my friends here; Malva to all the others. In my defense, I can assure you that I did not, of course, come up with this name myself. My father did that. Oh, you know him, the great poet. Just as he gave titles to his poems and poetry collections, he gave me a name; one that he himself never uttered in public. My eternal life started after my death in Gouda in 1943, where my funeral was attended by a small handful of people. Very different from my father's funeral, thirty years later in Santiago de Chile.

In a manner that would have been the envy of Socrates, my father passed away in the Santa Maria Hospital in Santiago after the staff managed to smother the hysteria that had overcome him on hearing of so much barbarous injustice that he, who had always been amiable and calm and able to keep a cool head even under the most horrendous circumstances, had flown into fits of rage and desperate screaming, in short: had ranted like one possessed, until finally the white-coated doctor arrived to calm him down with a sedative jab and the sweet slumber he sank into slipped-up massively, sloping down into infinity like an endless chute and my father felt the delicious descent tingle in his underbelly while actually rising up to the realms of the afterlife, where I will not meet him for a long time to come but where he has to be somewhere none the less, as the afterlife is large and besides, he was as dead as a doornail, or so the doctors concluded unanimously the next day from his stopped pulse and the indisputable fact that his eyes, too, stayed shut and nothing, absolutely nothing about him moved; not the faintest breeze stirred in those limbs, which were as stiff and motionless as if a solar eclipse and the dead of winter had set in suddenly and simultaneously.

I deliberately spun out the last sentence to give my father time, while it rambled on, to leave this life and enter death at his own pace.

His loss was felt most keenly by his widow, Matilde Urrutia. She bent over the dead man, kissed his hands, groped around on the floor next to his bed for the fountain pen that had slipped from his fingers, eventually spotted it out of reach when already kneeling with one arm stretched under the bed, gruffly asked the nurse for a broom to sweep the object toward herself and – mischievous, incorrigible Patoja – stuck it behind her ear under a casually tumbling lock of hair, resolving to use it later to copy out his memoirs before writing her own account of their life together.

Halfway on his lengthy journey to the realm of the dead, I decided to accompany my stiff-stolid father. I took the hand which he had used for writing during just about all his life, and for a little while, we floated over Santiago's smoldering rooftops together. The presidential palace, the park, the stadium, the slums full of laborers and the Mapocho River all lay far below us. My father saw not only his friends being tortured to death, but also the funeral procession accompanying him to his stone tomb, streaming through the streets down below like a living, human branch of the Mapocho, while countless corpses drifted down the river itself.

We heard the faraway battle cries coming from that direction, the Internationale, the cheering of the Communist Youth and, half carried away by the wind but still audible: "*¡Camarada Pablo Neruda! ¡Presente! ¡Ahora y siempre!*"

And all around, we saw spirits rise from the buildings, the stadium, the fields and the harbor, taking to the empty sky like us.

I doubt my father noticed me at his side, by the way, even though I was holding his hand all the time. He kept staring straight down as if trying to imprint every act of the human tragedy unfolding below us on his memory. Now and forever. The wind, a measure of his fever dream, seemed to have more grasp on him than on me; he started rising faster. So I let him go, staring after him for a while until he had disappeared from my view.

Federico was nowhere to be seen; neither were Salvador, Miguel or Víctor. No one from his exuberant, ever-expanding, never-thinning entourage, whose members came from all over the continent, indeed eventually the whole world, surrounding him wherever he went; not even a single one of his most devoted readers had turned up posthumously to attend my father's transition into the afterlife. And I kept asking myself why I, of all the dead who had known him, was the one allowed to see him off.

Now I understand it was so I would be able to tell you about it.

I was still marveling at the unstoppable flow of people appearing out of every corner of Santiago de Chile on September 25, 1973, to join my father's funeral procession, when, in the depth below, I suddenly spotted *your* father. You probably won't believe me, but honestly, Hagar: there he was, the tall Dutchman, in the middle of the swelling crowd of the living that had consisted of a couple of hundred people at first but had eventually grown into thousands. Why else do you think I chose you to tell my story to? He was on the alert. Notebook flipped open, he wrote down all he saw while at the same time taking great care not to be singled out by the sharp eye of one of the many *carabinieros*.

The notes he made that day have been preserved, written in the endearing homespun code language he used so he'd be able to save himself if he was arrested despite all caution, as had happened before in Bolivia. Several years earlier, under Ovando's dictatorship, he had languished in the prisons of La Paz and Oruro for three weeks under suspicion of having contact with *guerrilleros*. From my heavenly heights, I pored over the hieroglyphs your father was committing to paper at that moment in Chile, their meaning as clear as day to me the moment I saw them. I let his words sink in and then I let your father go, too, and glided on alone, following the funeral procession below me like a condor follows a colony of rabbits. There was Matilde again, la Patoja, walking along on her short legs: brave, determined and on the brink of being plunged into a deep grief that was starting to seep into her soul drop by drop, like the never-ending southern rain leaking through the hole in the zinc roof of her ramshackle parental home in Chillán.

;

Now this Patoja – the nickname my father had lovingly given the last of his three wives meant "little short-legs" in Chilean Spanish, though he used "Curly" and "Fuzzyhead" just as often – was anything but a fool! Her "fuzzyheadedness" only applied to her hairstyle, not, as in my case, her mind. The state of her hair being variable and entirely independent of the rest of her head, my father did not think of its fuzziness as a shortcoming; on the contrary, he found it endearing. When they woke up in the morning (while I lurked in a corner like a shadow, spying on their happiness) and he would ask her, "Lazy Patoja, how much longer are you going to sleep?," her copper tresses lay on the bed like straw and twigs lining their little love nest. The sight of him engrossed in fondling and caressing that creature's locks, twisting them around his finger, arranging them into outlandish shapes, would have been enough to move a medieval monk to utter the famous first words written in the Dutch language: "All the birds have started building nests, except for you and me. What are we waiting for?" Though waiting would have been pointless, anyway – my father and Matilde did not have any children together. I am the only offspring my father ever begot.

The reason my father loved la Patoja so much was of course that her hair was the color of copper, and copper is one of Chile's national products, and my father was mad about Chile. He had a love-hate relationship with the metal because it was in the hands of the Anaconda Copper Mining Company, who used every cent generated by the sale of this valuable metal to line its own, American, pockets. The poor Chileans, as meager as the northern desert soil itself, didn't earn a copper-colored cent from it. The nationalization of such thoroughly Chilean products snapped up by large foreign corporations, which had been set in motion so dynamically under the new regime, led to the coup. The multinationals, supported by the United States out of fear of another Cuba, brought the degenerate general to power, and the junta forced the democratically chosen socialist president Salvador Allende to take his own life – which, and I have to say this, directly or indirectly also resulted in the death of my father. In any case, this love-hate relationship did not affect his pure love for Matilde. While his first wife – my mother, a Dutchwoman from Batavia – was an eccentric foreigner, his second, dare-devil Delia, came from an Argentinian background already less exotic to my father, and when he finally hooked up with his last companion, she had the added benefit of being familiar with the poverty, the cold and the ceaseless rains of rural southern Chile.

Her coppery, homey smell and warmth must have been agreeable to him, as he let her bask in his famous embrace until death drove its own, black nail in its place. And now she feared that the death my father's sleep had slipped into so seamlessly was not a natural one.

No, not a drop of blood had been shed, not a spatter spilled! This death was so perfect, so clean, leaving no dirty smudges, making sure hands and fingers were immaculate afterwards so there was no proof of evil intent. Given that the calming jab my father had been administered so professionally by a white-coated doctor may well have been poison, the comparison of my father's death with that of the philosopher Socrates, who was handed a cup of hemlock for allegedly inciting the young to rebel against the government with his impudent but all too credible talk, is not as far-fetched as you might think. My father, too, was very possibly murdered for turning adolescents – as well as adults, by the way – against the government.

Even if it wasn't real poison, as those who excavated and examined my father's corpse in a different era believe to have determined, it was the venom of the times and of the events that eventually and unexpectedly killed my father, the great poet suffering from prostate cancer. This happened during the junta of General Augusto Pinochet, whose reign of terror in the Chile of the nineteen-seventies and eighties split the population into murderers on the one hand and martyrs on the other, with the ease of a coppersmith or a god forging his idols into different shapes in the heat of battle.

Pitiful Patoja, all alone in the world, my father's widow, tireless guardian of his dreams and status, would find herself the patron saint of my father's estate after his death. She would pass on the fruits of his pen to posterity. Former intellectual friends were all the happier to leave this job to her because, under this new regime, they suddenly wanted to distance themselves from that Communist of a Neruda, while I – the true fruit of flesh and blood though long since turned spirit – can do nothing but watch in envy as she takes command of his pages, leaving her mark of red nail varnish and sickly sweet perfume; denying and bad-mouthing any earlier and subsequent subjects of my father's passion, covering up any affairs he had behind her back that were just beginning to come to light, and praising the love between my father and herself to celestial heights.

So high is her praise for the love she shared with my father, it is even out of reach of the dead. I know that now, being dead myself, and writing as the daughter who was denied her father's love. But all-knowing as I am, I can't help admitting that Matilde Urrutia did a competent job of surreptitiously editing my father's memoirs, even though I don't get a single mention in them. Forgive me my two-facedness; it's very confusing to be dead and forgotten as well as alive and omniscient.

Incidentally, I'm writing all of this to you with my father's pen. I'll tell you how I came by it later.

TWO

THE MALVA, OR MALLOW, is a flower, a pretty flower, and the seashore mallow is a special flower because it grows on the Chilean coast, my father's favorite place. It is the reason my father chose this name for me, along with the fact that his mother was called Rosa, and giving his daughter the name of another flower was a way of paying tribute to her. He had never known her, because he was just two months old when she died, too weakened by labor to withstand an onslaught of tuberculosis. The stepmother who raised him and whom he gave the far more affectionate name mamadre, was called Trinidad Candia Marverde. He loved her so much, he wanted my name to refer to her too; Malva sounds remotely like Marverde, and Trinidad is my third given name.

Some people believe my father felt half-orphaned all his life, and that it prevented him from being a proper father. Whether this is true, I don't know. At any rate, I was named after the mallow. And I turned out as ugly as that flower is beautiful.

Do you know why a Dutch name for the mallow is "cheese weed"? The seeds that appear on this annual plant are shaped like tiny cheeses! Round with flattened sides, they look just like a wheel of genuine Gouda cheese. It so happens I was buried in Gouda back in 1943, and the shape of my head is exactly the same as that of the seeds dangling from the mallow. Surely even my father, the great poet, couldn't possibly have anticipated that when he decided to grace me with this name? The *Big Botany Book* says that the mallow looks as if it were intended for greatness but failed miserably somewhere on the way, and with that comment, the *Big Botany Book* hits the nail squarely on the head. Maybe I subconsciously copied the plant's behavior; maybe it became reality like a self-fulfilling prophecy. An even more appropriate name might have been that of the *Malva neglecta;* the mallow's plain stepsister, a kind of Cinderella among flowers. "Small cheese weed" is the charming Dutch name of the Malva neglecta; the English one is equally marvelous: Ignored mallow.

Echoing the Malva neglecta's white petals, the clothes I wore during my short existence on earth consisted of gossamer white dresses and a knitted white cap. This even made me look like a flower, my head an overgrown calyx hidden behind the petals. Could anything be more fitting for a girl who died from water on the brain aged eight, who in life was rejected by her Chilean father, a poet, and who is buried in Gouda? The mallow has a short flowering season. It often grows on the side of the road, like a weed. Weeds are known for being indestructible, and therefore having eternal life.

;

Despite the transparency of my ghostly frame, talking to you has made me blush, I can feel it. You, who are writing all this down for me, can't see it, but I know my flushed cheeks are glowing with zeal. I realize that the power of the pen is running away with us, and can almost feel myself come alive again as I surrender to the inspiration of its twists and turns like tracks carved on ice by figure skaters. I let the exquisite swollenness welling up inside sweep me away. My chest is expanding as if it were filling up with oxygen again, carrying me to my father after all. But I have to take care not to stumble over my words. I have so much to tell about the time I spent on earth with no language at my disposal, and about now, the moment I want to communicate everything that is preying on my mind.

Me! A narrator! Omniscient! Ha ha! If my father could hear that, he'd cry out, "Don't make me laugh!" Does he even remember what I looked like on earth? He knew me until I was about two years old. In letters, not meant for publication, he called me "a three-kilo vampire, a leech, a freak, the monster, *un ser perfectamente ridículo*, a perfectly ridiculous being," because of my puny little body and my enormous head. He – the king of language – called me a "semicolon"!

Of course I realize he never really meant any of it, that there was no real hostility in the words he addressed with such apparent casualness to a beautiful blonde, but that he was feigning the kind of ironic indifference so sought-after in men by women of a certain age and beauty. In any case, he did me a favor, and I say that now without a trace of irony. I'm grateful to him for that last characterization; after all, the semicolon is my favorite punctuation mark; half period, half comma, it is the most ambiguous punctuation mark there is, and therefore the most universally applicable.

My father's description of me as a "perfectly ridiculous being" is highly ambiguous, as perfect ridiculousness is a paradox; the ridiculous is imperfect by definition. But I was so very ridiculous that my ridiculousness had reached perfection.

The semicolon is the ultimate symbol of ambivalence; combining the absoluteness of the period on the one hand with the comma of continuance on the other, its duplicity mirrors the duplicity of life itself, and my feelings toward my genitors; in me, their two versions come together which, though mutually exclusive, are nevertheless equally valid because both have lived, and both must therefore be done justice.

The period, of course, represents death, but the comma shows there's more to come, moderates the period; while the period curbs the comma's freewheelingness, stabilizes it.

If it were up to the comma, the end would never come; each comma would be followed by the next, and so on to infinity. And the period would make short work of everything too soon. Standing completely alone, the period would become too certain of itself. The period and comma in the semicolon are like yin and yang, like opposites united in a single symbol, and there is always a dot of white in the black, just as there is a dash of black in the white because nothing is definite, nothing absolute.

The semicolon may be replaced by the words "in short," which is also a reference to measurement. In short, a better punctuation mark isn't known to me, who am tied to so many laws of numbers and measures, simultaneously immured by and immune to them, that this mark really seems tailor-made for me. With this in mind, I consider my earthly frame a blessing, which as my father pointed out has the characteristic shape of the semicolon; my small body a comma, a crooked stroke, a twisted worm, and my ever-expanding skull a grotesque period rising above itself and growing toward heaven; toward this one vast afterlife heaven that has taken me in, despite everything.

;

Now that hardly anyone knows how to use it any more, the semicolon is threatened with extinction, placing it at a disadvantage compared to the other punctuation marks just as I, as a human being, was inferior to my peers.

What is more, the semicolon's task is to stand somewhere in the middle of a sentence, with text before and after. The semicolon is a gateway, a funnel, as it were; what comes before, is repeated afterwards in a shorter but more succinct way. Or vice versa: the short remark that went before is smeared out afterwards, described and illustrated at length. The part after the semicolon is actually a summary of the sweeping claims made earlier. Or else the illustrated version of the rough sketch that went before.

That is exactly my role up here! Like the condor, who according to Andes mythology feeds on putrid carrion on earth before rising up to the mountaintops – the seat of the gods and omniscient spirits – as a messenger between the gods and the earth, I represent the gateway between the sad life that went before my death and the beautiful story I made of it afterwards; like a short but concise summary, or an extensive but highly relevant footnote. And I do it all for my father, who denied me in life. So that he should know. Or if not he, then the rest of the world.

I am suddenly overcome by a sense of shame. I'm reminded of something a friend of mine here once said to me: that I'm post-humously trying to butter up my father, and that it is a ridiculous, fruitless endeavor. Daniel said that, you'll meet him later. He said I'd been fooling myself the whole time. It would all come to nothing. He doesn't believe I'll ever win back my father's love. It's clutching at straws, this posthumous consciousness; it's a giant ruse to put off the moment I have to face the fact that what's done cannot be undone, and that I played no part in my father's life. I will never get any closer to him, ever. Not even now, in death. The eternal insight I have been granted here is only fuelling my self-deception, and that's why it is time I said goodbye to my father, just as his brand-new widow was forced to do. All right, all right, I'll do it.

;

But first, let me continue my story. Now I've gotten hold of "the pen,"

I'm not about to let go of it again.

I drew the comparison between my father and Socrates for another reason. Difficult as it is to understand that, in the world's first democracy, the philosopher was handed a cup of poison merely for speaking his mind, it must be just as incomprehensible that a poet who took such pride in his compassion for the underprivileged could have rejected and concealed his own daughter because of her disfigurement.

My father's memoirs, published by his widow after his death, were titled *I Confess, I Have Lived.*

He had, yes.

And her own: *My Life with Pablo Neruda.*

Her life, yes! Hers! Oh, and all that about nail polish and sickly sweet perfumes isn't true, by the way; as I now know, she was more partial to beds of roses.

Listen. One evening, shortly before my death, la Patoja and my father agreed that I would not be mentioned.

It went like this: she is sitting at his sickbed. In a neutral voice, as if merely making a suggestion for the arrangement of a bunch of flowers, she whispers, "Malva?"

He looks at her for a few moments, countless thoughts racing through his mind, but eventually drops his eyes. And so my father, once bread and earth to my hands and feet, who had been everything that existed between me and the horizon, everything I strained to reach from my cradle, now reduced the horizon to a range of directions in which to shake his head (I watched the countermovement of his cheeks like a visual echo) when asked whether he would mention the existence of his daughter in his memoirs. He had been to every point on the compass his rotating head faced that evening; he'd had the whole horizon, and more.

THREE

MY PARENTS WERE MARRIED in Batavia on December 6, 1930. My mother looked like an albatross in the pleated white skirt that billowed around her hips and with her wide-brimmed white hat. The resemblance was not lost on my father, who loved albatrosses. Thinking of the albatross of Baudelaire, he fully expected the large, ungainly woman to be lifted up by wings of passion and fly gracefully through the skies of the future with him at her side. And later, much later, on their retreat from Batavia and the long sea journey that accompanied it (the grey-brown water in the wake of their ship like the filthy train of a wedding dress, seagulls jeering after them), the image of the albatross came back to him. It was no longer Baudelaire's albatross, however, but Coleridge's, the docile bird the Ancient Mariner shot down because its ever-circling movements – constantly winging around him, always too close – had started grating on his nerves.

But on that afternoon on the 6th of December, as the sun lay their shadows at their feet, that albatross was not even a speck in the distance yet. They were still wrapped up in the small trivialities of daily life, such as having their wedding photograph taken (oh, if only that hopeful moment had been allowed to last as long as their immortalised image). A hand's breadth taller than my father, who himself stood almost six feet tall, my mother was obliged to bend her knees a little – which is probably why she seems to be clinging to him for dear life.

Gossiping contemporaries and prejudiced later biographers alike have described her embrace as possessive, "as if she has finally bagged him, her big fish, the consul!" The sharp tongues of the Batavian bourgeoisie had been wagging like this for many centuries.

My mother couldn't wait to leave that suffocating environment behind her as quickly as possible, *and* with a brand new husband she doted on. She carried his photograph with her all the time. Wherever she went, she would crow to whoever she met, "He's a consul! A real consul!"

My father never resembled his own father, the awkward freight train driver, more than at that moment; as if the whole wedding had only been arranged for the benefit of my grandfather in Temuco. Standing meekly on the arm of his spouse, his face was as inscrutable as a Javanese mask.

My grandfather himself came from Belen, short for Bethlehem; an unsightly village in the southernmost part of Chile, untraceable on any map. In the middle of the forest, sandwiched between the ocean and an impenetrable mountain range, stood the cradle of the Reyes family, whose offspring, with such grotesque names as Amós, Oseas, Joel and Abadías, already carried the stamp of archaism; born out of secrecy, scandal and taboos, they were so backward, boorish and ignorant that the forest was more of a refuge and a mother to them than a recreation area.

Why do you think my grandfather attached so much importance to my father's respectability; because he himself never achieved it, of course! One of my father's brothers was the son of my grandfather and the woman who would later become my father's stepmother, but had been conceived by this future stepmother before my father's birth; and to complicate things even further, my father's sister was also the daughter of said stepmother, but from another man. Even if there had been a simple explanation, no one was allowed to breathe a word about it.

Hiding from all those unresolved and unmentionable lapses which forced him to walk on eggshells at home so as not to detonate his father's explosive temper, my father fled into the forest. There, he gazed at the beetles and flowers, hidden gems in the dusty sunlight sifting down through the dense foliage, creating a space for him in which to lose himself in contemplation and drift away into daydreams.

It was there that the first verses blossomed out of his breast and his heart swelled up to melancholy greatness.

;

I can see him sitting there now, a little boy in the vast forest where a ray of sunshine falling on his hand has just revealed poetry to him. He feels the outside world resonate inside of him. How is it possible that he, this creator, so in touch with his environment, should produce a freak?

;

If my father's brother and sister were a taboo subject, I, his daughter, was an even greater one. So little was known of me that the *Who's Whos* of world literature, if they mentioned me at all in the endless entries dedicated to my father, could only hazard occasional wild guesses about me. Most of them omitted me altogether; some falsely claimed I suffered from Down's syndrome; others, equally mistakenly, that I was killed during an air raid in the Second World War in Europe, and on the rare occasions they made mention of my mother, they misspelled her name with blithe indifference:

Antonieta María Aagenar Vogelzanz instead of Maria Antoinette Hagenaar (Marietje, for short; and the last name was supposed to be Vogelzang, my grandmother's surname, though of course maternal surnames are not used in Dutch).

All other things concerning my father have been carefully documented. More than enough has been written about them, so I will save myself the trouble of repeating such profiles. Instead, I'll tell you about my mother's family, who are as yet completely unknown (I want to infuse every fibre of each letter with my loyalty-driven sense of equality; I will let it sink to the level of the comma and make it soar to the peaks of the Andes).

;

My mother once won a magic lantern in a school competition in the Dutch East Indies. For weeks afterwards, she and her brothers were glued to the fairy tale scenes projected on the wall like a modern-day, Western *wayang* performance. Traveling back in time, I have tried penetrating that shadow world to warn her of the dangers looming on the horizon, but every time the dark shadow I cast over her future made her cry a little, my grandmother came in to tell her not to be afraid; that it was only a children's toy.

My mother's family had settled in the area two hundred years earlier. It all began when our ancestor, the future governor-general of the Dutch East Indies, Jeremias van Riemsdijk (Utrecht, 1712 – Batavia, 1777), left Delft on board the *Proostwijk* on February 25, 1735, and crossed the ocean to the East Indies, where he embarked on a lightning career at the VOC Dutch East Indian Company. He made sure his nine-year-old son, my grandfather's great-great-grandfather, was put on the VOC payroll, fortunately without expecting the boy to lift a finger in return, and by doing so set a new trend and secured the family's capital for future generations.

My mother's illustrious ancestor was so wealthy he had a glass coach shipped in from Europe, drawn by glossy Arab thoroughbreds, in which he went on jaunts along the paddy fields to watch his two hundred male and female slaves laboring away. Jeremias van Riemsdijk married five times, and each of his wives was Eurasian. The family was typical for its matriarchal hierarchy, which was becoming commonplace among high-ranking colonial VOC families at the time. In generations to come, power was passed down the female line, though the wealthy women did not profit much from this; all they did was bear a succession of rulers who remained, to all intents and purposes, in command. My great-grandmother finally broke through this pattern; after the death of her husband, a clergyman, she successfully applied for permission from the Ministry of Colonies for her son, an engineer, and herself to construct a railway for steam and electric trams in Java and Borneo, and to carry out a geological survey to determine if the area was suitable for mining.

It was also somewhere down this slightly less wealthy female line that my mother acquired the drop of Malay blood, which so enthralled my father, from a local slave with a beautiful name: Oranina Bloemenstina. She was the daughter of Oranina van Batavia, also a slave, who is recorded in the family genealogy as being "insane"; though it is easy to imagine what brought about this all too readily applied and eventually self-fulfilling stigma of madness: colliding cultures, discrimination and oppression.

Although the overall fortune of the Van Riemsdijks diminished considerably down the generations as the VOC lost its wealth – particularly in my mother's line, which had already been apportioned a smaller part of the inheritance because of its descent from the "insane" slave – my mother's parents were very well off at first.

Thanks to his lineage, nationality, name and connections and, above all, my great-grandmother's help, my maternal grandfather was made managing director, deputy manager and majority shareholder of various mining companies in Java and Borneo. In the long run, however, he wasn't able to hold his own among the other colonists. The place was crawling with easily offended egos, short fuses and very volatile tempers. He was taken to court several times, first for insulting some respectable gentleman or other, then again for crossing coffee company directors by writing articles showing that the cultivation of coffee near Palembang was doomed to failure. After the death of his beloved mother he made some bad investments, wiping out the last remnant of the family capital.

Then one day, we now write the year 1905, a bailiff came to confiscate his white cotton shirt and trousers, as the East Indian papers reported gleefully and without passing up the opportunity to make a sly dig at his giant stature (the tallness he passed on to my mother).

It was the beginning of the end for my grandfather, and the end of the glory of our branch of the Van Riemsdijk family. My grandfather had always been a very erudite man, and a renowned expert on coffee plant diseases. He had worked as an editor for the *Indische Cultuuralmanak*, which through the years had published countless of his contributions. Now, even his letters to the editor were rejected, and on March 5, 1920, on the exact day my mother turned twenty, he suddenly collapsed and lay dead on the floor.

Palm trees swaying benevolently in the wind, the seemingly deep-rooted calm of three centuries of colonization that was as torpid as the heat, the ayahs in the yard, and behind the balustrades only the rhythm of rocking chairs and idleness; at barely twenty years of age, my mother had to wave goodbye to her cushy personal life, toodle-oo to *tempo dulu*, the good old days, gone before the rest of the colony even cottoned on, though some of the balustrades were already broken and the legs of the colonials' rocking chairs getting rickety.

And to make matters worse, neither of her brothers returned from an expedition to Malang a year later. From that moment on, my mother was condemned to living with my exceptionally hard-put grandmother, who had lost her husband as well as both her sons before the age of forty-two. The responsibility to uphold the family's reputation now lay wholly on my mother's shoulders. A good-looking, sensible girl, as was expected of girls in that century, she made a living working as a secretary at the British Trading House. Her wages were remarkably high for that era: the equivalent of three hundred Swiss francs a month. It was more than she would earn in her married life (nothing) or after being abandoned (a pittance), but her social position waned with each passing year; she had almost given up hope of finding her savior, the man who would change everything by marrying her.

;

Eventually, the man did come. Having left his parents' house in Temuco to study in the Chilean capital Santiago, he who would be my father cut a dashing figure in the black cape his own father had worn as a freight train driver, and, in order to mislead aforementioned parent who would have flown into a rage at seeing his poems, published his work under the pseudonym Pablo Neruda instead of his own name, Ricardo Eliécer Neftalí Reyes Basoalto.

So much has been written about my father's early life already that I'm going to limit myself here to a quick and sloppy summary, reeled off in a bored drone: he joined several student associations, became an editor of a student literary journal and published articles in it, made friends, had his first erotic adventures, lived in a room with a print on the wall that showed an admired English poet shortly after committing suicide, and was melancholy and cheerful in turns, just as countless other students at the time, before, and since, but with the great difference that he made a name for himself as a poet. Keen to leave, he managed to secure a diplomatic post, picking a spot on the map he didn't know, somewhere in a random dent in the globe selected for its rolling name, and left for the capital of Burma, Rrrrrrrrrrrrrrrrrrangoon!

My father chose this destination out of a refusal to conform, at a time when every self-respecting Latin American was headed for the cultural mecca of Paris. Can it really be a coincidence, Hagar, that your father, out of sheer non-conformity like mine, chose Latin America as the destination of his first travels as a sociology student and aspiring journalist?

FOUR

IN YOUR MOTHER'S LIVING ROOM was a cabinet with heavy sliding doors, and in the cabinet a pile of papers and press cuttings. It was a large pile, grey and grimy, printed in black ink that stained your fingers. The thin, rustling paper was densely printed, but you were not old enough to read yet.

"What's that?"

"Your father's news stories." The words your father wrote into his diary later returned as newspaper articles and ended up in your home, where you dwelled in the various hollows of your apartment like an exotic jungle creature; the underside of the orange woollen sofa was a dark cave whose frayed fringe swished like vines. Underneath the heavy table made of railway sleepers: the inside of a hollow tree, a place of refuge. The mantelpiece: a lookout. Cushions: rocks; windows: skies; ornaments: stars; cupboards: thicket; beds: rafts, and sometimes hideouts. Rush mats: earth. Carpet tiles: oceans.

Through the wisps and fog banks of time, like messages in a bottle flung at random into an unknown sea, your father's articles washed up on the shore of your upstairs apartment in Amsterdam.

You would often sit on the ledge above the radiator, fantasizing about your absent father and his urge for freedom. You took a hand mirror from one of the shelves, but instead of holding it to your face, you tilted it up toward the ceiling. A white, infinitely empty floor appeared in the depth beneath your feet. It was like floating in a vacuum. If you dodged the occasional lampshade sprouting out of the floor from nowhere like an enormous flower, you had an otherwise empty ballroom at your disposal that led, at its other end, to the door of your room, where you could lose yourself in your reveries.

;

I follow the inner eye of your childhood imagination at full gallop, bolting across the hunting grounds, which I am now, in death, allowed to ride over for all eternity; and as I watch life on earth, long past, unfold on the sweeping acres of land on either side, I spot him a second time.

Just ahead of me. On horseback. And though we are going at a gallop, the past, which never actually passes at all, catches up with us. It is July 1, 1970, and we're riding over the plains of the Argentinian pampas. There, towering over his friend B., is the imposing figure of the man who will become your father in just two years' time.

That morning, the two of them were shaken ruthlessly from their sleep by a certain Patsy, wife of the English large landowner Layman, who had put them up for the night. She won't give them a moment's respite – the train is about to leave and they haven't even breakfasted yet. Your father ends up missing the train anyway, because his travel companion is so lazy, he had to be woken up with a wet sponge. Luckily, the next train is due thirty minutes later, and they are soon carried through the beautiful morning countryside (the *cordillera* mauve and many other colors) across dried-up river beds dotted with people shoveling stones for the iron factory. Layman introduces them to the manager; an army major, as this is a military factory.

Yet again, the two near-hippies – your father and his friend – are rubbing shoulders with representatives of a tier of society that should by rights be closed to them, but who are outdoing each other in amiableness and hospitality when it comes to paying bills and writing letters of recommendation for these two young protégés of the Old Boy's Club. Your father suspects that identification plays a part in it – that their hosts wish they could have traveled like that when they were young and strong enough to do so – and he takes full advantage of their vicarious need. It sometimes feels whorish, the way he pays for the hospitality offered by the bored old upper-class gentlemen and their wives on their remote *latifundios* with High-Minded Conversation. More than once, your father acts the part of "Goofy in the guise of a Society Gentleman," and it occurs to him that the fact he is never the one who ends a conversation may well be the key to his recent successes.

The two young sociology students and budding journalists (business cards with *"estudiantes viajeros"* in their horseback-pummelled back pockets) are further rewarded with information that interests them keenly, for Layman & co. takes them on a tour of the entire factory and furnace – so close to the various manufac-turing processes, they constantly run the risk of getting burned. They learn that day laborers regularly fall into crevices, niches or machines, in which case the factory, mining company or plantation pay for the funeral at best; the wife and children left behind can forget about any other form of compensation.

Your father jots it down with deep contempt, becoming an irritant instead of a valued guest to his hosts the moment he detects any "capitalist tendencies," at which the High-Minded Conversations are soon cut short and the students dismissed with fresh letters of recommendation in their pockets.

But for now, Layman just scratches behind his ear and, ever the gentleman, takes your father and his friend to lunch at the casino. A "delicious lunch," according to your father, and for the umpteenth time, the world is treated to the spectacle of two gentlemen squabbling for the privilege of settling the bill while your father and his traveling companion look the other way and pretend not to notice.

A special chauffeur drives them to the mine. They stopped on the way for some horseback riding, which is where I met them. They simply climbed on the backs of a couple of horses standing ready, galloped like the wind and lost the race to the major's young son. As it later turned out, a saddle had been loose; yet another close shave! The views are beautiful, surreal landscapes of charcoal furnaces standing in long rows, and on arrival at the top of the hill they are met by a man your father refers to as a "fat old codger"; a kind of foreman the other workers call "engineer." Next, they go down the mine in full collier's kit. A lorry takes them to the entrance. The driver is a quirky German man who is predictably delighted with their visit and immediately has a special wagon coupled to the back of the ore train for the two hippies to sit in – on planks of wood to keep them from getting dirty.

Hasta el fondo, con autorización, as the Kraut said, your father is thinking.

;

Forty years later, he'll tell you, "At the time, the height of flower power, everyone traveled to Afghanistan and India to smoke hashish and feel the vibes, so I wanted to go in the opposite direction. If others went east, I would go west. It was more interesting there politically, too; all that touchy-feely stuff left me cold. With hindsight, I've come to understand that my constant refusal to conform was a result of the Second World War: being the son of a

Jewish father half of whose family had been murdered in the war taught me that crowds are dangerous, and that the only way of escaping the potential danger of a crowd is making sure to do things slightly differently from others. I interviewed old Mr. Oesterman, who opened my eyes: a Jew, he had escaped the concentration camp by always dragging his feet, hiding, going the other way; doing the exact opposite from everyone else. That's why I became an expert on Latin America."

FIVE

NON-CONFORMISM also led *my* father, a student and the same age your father was when he went to Latin America, to Rangoon, where he, in turn resembling Rimbaud, experienced his own season in hell before traveling on to Ceylon, Singapore and Java.

And so, after many wanderings and failed love affairs, he met my future mother on the last island, where he made the mistake of finally giving in to the expectations of others.

My father was born to roam the globe and to sing, it was a fact he was instinctively all but certain of, and one he propagated from the moment he was able to reach the pen (on the tips of his toes, tongue between his teeth, there, on his father's table, that pen, that pen). He wanted to travel the world singing, and he did. Others detested him because they could tell he was different, and just for a moment – one single instant of his life – he changed tack; he complied with the demands of his environment, and adapted. The idiot! Working as a consul in Batavia at the time, he just had to go and get married (it was what the other consuls wanted; only then would they take him seriously, which in turn was what my grandfather, who didn't take him seriously either because of his poetic outpourings, wanted). The idiot, I repeat.

After the sudden death of her father and both her brothers, my future mother was so thrilled to have a man in her life again – and one who would bring with him her long hoped-for promotion to married woman, to boot – that she clapped her hands together, clasping his between them, and lavished just the dose of unconditional affection and devotion on him that he had missed so sorely in his years of solitary diplomatic service.

The matter was soon clinched.

My parents married in a fit of tropical madness.

No, that's not entirely true! Carried away by a pen that wants to go faster than me, and by my impatience to tell the whole story, I've ended up warping reality.

;

He was genuinely in love, but with two others who were out of his reach. Teresa was the name of the first, but he called her Terusa, the pet name he would later secretly model my mother's name on, kneading it into something he was able to pronounce: Marietje became Maruca.

This Terusa, then, was a little too headstrong for a puppy love. His other love interest, also with too much of a mind of her own, was called Albertina, a city girl and fellow student from Santiago.

He met Terusa when her parents took her to the same seaside town he was visiting, the place where he had discovered the sea as a boy, and there, on the coast, witnessed only by the blossoming mallow, he had loved her deeply and fervently; it was there his first love awakened and immediately embedded itself into his chest like a hook, which the absence and distance that inevitably followed only drove in deeper, as if absence and yearning had become equivalent to love itself. A dangerous reading of the situation, as it would mean that the presence of the loved one would in turn drive away love. Accordingly, my mother's availability would eventually make her redundant.

Albertina and Teresa: his two unreachable muses; his muses, precisely because both were unavailable. They were the real-life objects of his desire on whom he based Marisol and Marisombra in his *Veinte poemas de amor y una canción desesperada*, the collection of poems that had already brought my father fame in Chile and in all of Latin America by the time he met my mother in Java. Granted, the two characters also represent other women and girls (yes all right, many other women and many other girls), but Albertina and Teresa were the ones he longed for most – and he went on pining for his muses, persevering in his proposals and threatening each of them separately, in much the same words and almost identical love letters, that if they turned him down, he would marry someone else.

My mother just happened to be in the right place at the right time for the threat to be carried out. That is what this classic, ultimately simple tale boils down to. It was even worse than just conformism and tropical madness; it was the equally dangerous as banal cocktail of loneliness and convenience.

She was more respectable than Josie Bliss, the Burmese femme fatale he had been forced to break up with shortly before when their affair all but ended fatally, and who was also still gnawing at his heart with venomous teeth, leaving a scar that would never fade, not even in the caring hands of his winsome, obliging and oh so virtuous wife. He put her to work writing letters to his parents, a task she undertook with great devotion as part of her marital duties, and these epistles written in her competent Spanish have been preserved and came to my attention long after my death to bear witness against all the prejudiced biographers who claimed my mother had only herself and her supposed aloofness to blame for my father leaving her.

;

Alas, if his own father didn't think much of poetry, neither did Teresa's parents; just as little, in fact, as Albertina's.

Albertina Azócar: if it weren't for the sake of bitter reality, I wouldn't even mention that syrupy-sweet name! She was a student at the time, and didn't want to drop out of university for him. But the dean had opened and read my father's love letters to her, and out of sheer anger she hit back, harming no one but herself, by giving up the course she had almost completed.

Later (when it was far too late for the drama to be undone and my father had already emerged as a wealthy and successful poet), she admitted that her rejection of him had been strongly influenced by her parents, who suspected him to be anything but a suitable husband. Poets were not held in high regard by potential parents-in-law in Chile in those days. Most were thought of as womanizers driven by excessive sexual urges, many as good-for-nothings weighed down by depression and poverty, all as reeking alcoholics – in short, an exceedingly bad bet to safeguard the future of one's own flesh and blood.

Oh, if only my grandmother had been as quick to form such well-founded prejudices against my father when he courted her daughter as the far more sensible parents of the other objects of his affection! If she had, the fatal mistake that was my parents' marriage might just have been avoided.

But you know how it goes: the title of consul sounded reassuring, and since just about anything was considered good enough for my doomed mother after the death of her father and brothers, this interesting foreigner (of the classic tall-dark-stranger-type whose appearance fortune tellers routinely predict to lovelorn women) seemed to have more to offer than she, at the spinsterish age of thirty, was entitled to hope for. And so, everyone around her started dropping subtle and not-so-subtle hints to the effect that she should count herself lucky with such a husband – even if his appearance was perfectly in line with expectations raised by her respectable VOC family tree – only to gossip behind her back about the "big fish" she had finally caught, and I am giving you such a detailed account of this story in the hope that its message might still get through to my mother and retroactively prevent her from making her mistake.

Teresa eventually married a typewriter repairman. That's right: while my father had become the proud owner of three magnificent houses and was considered Latin America's best-loved poet, the love of his life, forced to reject him because of his poor prospects, married a man who repaired the typewriters on which anaemic would-be poets copied out my father's love verses in their attic rooms in foredoomed attempts to win the hearts of girls who would in turn reject them by order of their meddling parents.

This pattern was to repeat itself countless times, though Teresa's parents and Teresa herself probably came to see their huge mistake eventually, just as Albertina and her parents were gnashing their teeth in regret. Though my father's love poems did – albeit secretly – help the two women to view their spouses in a more desirable light. Teresa gradually learned to think of the long, thin fingers with which her husband repaired typewriters as the slender hands of a pianist, and take pleasure in listening to the harsh music he produced when he was at work.

;

And that is how I see her now: Teresa, who always remained his Terusa in her heart, bathing in the morning light that falls in through the window onto her and her husband. He is seated at the typewriter; she is standing behind him with her hands on his shoulders, grim and wistful, hearing in the rattling noise the sounds my father whispered into her ear in the two most romantic nights of her life.

;

Teresa and Albertina; Marisol and Marisombra; if only those two meek lambs, or one of them at least, had mustered the courage to go against their parents' foolish, prejudiced opposition – the happy bride would have been happy indeed, as my father would have loved her more than he ever loved my mother. He would have heaped ode after ode on her, just to please her. My mother would not have gone down in history as my father's only lover to whom he never wrote a single love poem. I would not have existed. And neither would this book, though that would not have mattered as the need for writing it would, in the absence of so much tragedy and human misunderstanding, have vanished with it.

It would have been the best of all possible worlds: one in which there was no pride, prejudice or fear, and I would not have been born. But it was in this marriage that I was conceived. The moral of the story is that my parents' mismatch was the result of their individual miseries, and out of this misguided union came an even greater mistake: a misfit, namely me.

SIX

I'VE MADE SOME FRIENDS up here since my death, one of them Oskar Matzerath; you know him, the droll dwarf with the tin drum from the novel by Günter Grass. Then there's Lucia (James Joyce's daughter and a supposed schizophrenic) and Daniel (the son of Arthur Miller; Down syndrome).

Look at us, the unwholesome foursome, sitting obediently around a table; drooling a little into our food. Others are seated at the long tables, not drooling as much, but eating too. But we, the hoodwinked, have occupied the only round table in the dining room so we can turn our backs on the rest of the company, whispering and messing with our food while occasionally delivering kicks to each other under the table with the disjointed movements of the abnormal that are so typical of us. Do you remember how your mother used to say that in hell everyone eats alone, while in heaven each person feeds the one next to them? So where does that leave us, sitting at a table together but wielding our own cutlery?

It's one of those evenings when the cosmic light is exceptionally bright and the weather calm and unchanging and there is so little wind we can talk to each other in a relaxed whisper, which is what we like doing most, using as little breath as possible, even less than would be needed to blow out the flame of a candle. All of a sudden, the figure of the Polish poet Wisława Szymborska, whom we worship and I secretly aspire to make my grandmother, appears in the dining room.

Just like Oskar's father and mine, Szymborska is a Nobel laureate. But that's not the only reason I think of her so highly (and so does Oskar, by the way, though he denies it). I'm far more impressed by her infinite wisdom and engaging personality. For example, she wants nothing to do with biographers and wouldn't dream of writing her autobiography: she believes her poems speak for themselves, and that not too much should be read into her personality. A welcome contrast to my father's bulky memoirs, if you ask me. That's why I would like her to be my legal grandmother here, in the afterlife. I haven't had the courage to ask her yet. Every time he spots her, Oskar jabs my buttocks with his drumsticks, and poking me in her direction, smarms, "Come on! Ask her! Ask her!" He really is a tiresome pest, but I'm fond of him for reasons I don't quite understand myself.

As it is, all I have dared ask her about is my true nature and inner being. Szymborska, who has written so much poetry about the nature of the world and the beings living in it, is an expert on the subject, and I, forever struggling with the question of how I relate to a nature I emerged from but which has turned its back on me, am fervently hoping she will endorse my new self-image; it would posthumously lend my deformed frame a certain grandeur.

Practicing with Matzerath a couple of times, I haven't been able to utter more than a feeble stammer. In spite of this and with a pounding heart, I now step forward. "Tell me honestly, dear Wisława," I ask in far too soft a voice, while Oskar watches me prancing weightlessly toward the old lady on little hoofed feet, frivolously flapping my fan of make-believe feathers. "Wouldn't you agree I actually belong to the realm of mermaids, fauns and angels?"

Oskar strikes up a drumroll. Both of us wait with bated breath. The drumroll builds up, but Szymborska keeps her lips tightly shut.

We can hear chimeras and the rest of the mythical menagerie growl approvingly, weaving their eagle's beaks, dog's heads and bat's snouts from side to side and wagging their lion's tails.

"So you think," she says at last, almost as softly as I did, "I mean *you* when I say,

> you with your Devonian tail fins and alluvial breasts,
> your fingered hands and cloven feet,
> your arms alongside, not instead of, wings,
> your, heaven help us, diphyletic skeletons,
> your ill-timed tails, horns sprouted out of spite,
> illegitimate beaks, this morphogenic potpourri, those
> finned or furry frills and furbelows, the couplets
> pairing human/heron with such cunning
> that their offspring knows all, is immortal, and can fly."

"Yes, dearest Wisława," I say. "Wouldn't you agree that, with hindsight, I should be counted among that group of creatures rather than among common terrestrial mortals?"

The old Polish woman looks me up and down in silence and I can see emotion flickering in her eyes, but then she shakes her head vehemently, emphasising that such beings originated exclusively in the imagination and cannot exist on earth, that this is exactly what makes the human imagination so magnificent, so elevating; that it is the only thing capable of creating such non-viable creatures and bringing them to life, even if exclusively in the realm of fantasy. For just imagine if they, too, lived on earth:

> " – you must admit that it would be a nasty joke,
> excessive, everlasting, and no end of bother,
> one that mother nature wouldn't like and won't allow."

Daniel, Oskar and Lucia (like the deaf man, the blind man and the cripple), shrug (as if in unison). But the chimeras put their heads on their front paws and start whining softly.

What Szymborska is saying, is that there is limited scope for the existence of fauns, angels and mermaids, as they constitute an excess that mother nature wouldn't like and won't allow. The only problem is: whether nature likes it or not, this excess does exist; and I cry out, stirred up by Oskar's drumroll:

"Yes she does, Wisława, just look at us!"

The chimeras lift their heads with a start. I shout it with the little power my lungs can muster, but at the top of my voice nevertheless, because I am bewildered and want everyone around us to understand me. I am even counting on their approval. Still intimidated by the more able-bodied spirits around me, I jump at hearing my own voice, but ever since I've started telling you my story, my confidence has soared.

Like a self-elected spokesperson, I claim, "You're completely forgetting us, the mutants, the semi-snouted, double-billed, tripple-footed; the Cyclops, the giants and the dwarfs with their tin drums. We exist all right, but are condemned to beating the drum in the wings at every performance on the Stage of Life; where those who do have a part to play are giving their all; tirelessly; war after war, scandal after scandal. We are the audience, the witnesses. There is nothing else we can be."

SEVEN

I WAS CONCEIVED IN Buenos Aires, in 1933. Think tango, clinking glasses, marital rows, chunky chandeliers and a 90-metre skyscraper (the tallest residential building in the city, only just completed), "El Safico" on number 456 Avenida Corrientes, "the street that never sleeps." Here, on the twentieth floor, my future parents settled after staying in Santiago in the thirties, when the consulate in the Dutch East Indies was all but shut down because of the economic crisis. From this skyscraper, they had a spectacular view of the city and its picturesque skies, under which the street, at the speed of public transport and the accelerated revolving doors that gave entrance to the shops, propelled trade for those with money and even faster for those with none who were attracted by the hope of getting some: the prostitutes, pimps and other poor wretches that featured in the resounding tangos.

Up there, my father-to-be caught wistful evening glimpses of the sunsets he had described in his first collection of poems, *Crepusculario*. Looking out from his tower room on Maruri Street in Santiago de Chile, where he lived as a student, he had captured (this was years before meeting my mother) the most magnificent evening skies, threaded with golden rays of sunlight, woven through with yellow mist, shreds of orange and a dull red luster.

Now, the most flamboyant of sunrises and sunsets were again taking place behind the window panes, stirring no other emotion in my future mother, according to him, than one that drew loud oohs and aahs from her, as if taking her cue from him, confirming him in his awe instead of feeling it herself.

Stay out of my emotions, he said in his mind, where he also compared his own, melancholy, soul to a carrousel in the twilight and hers to a swing at an ordinary funfair. He had already stopped trying to hide his marital problems, though he sometimes half-heartedly kicked them under the carpet, only for them to peek out again the moment visitors arrived. Irritated, he went down the twenty flights of stairs to venture into the throng on nocturnal Corrientes. That's where it all happened, that's where his friends were waiting, where there were bars, the tinkling strumpets wearing their – to his mind – wonderfully sultry bells; and the moment he arrived at the ground floor, hands in his coat pockets, heart beating in the cool rhythm of the taxis' horns, he felt the world boil in his blood. At the bottom of the stairs, having descended into the underworld, my future father arose from his personal death.

But she, whom his friends called his *carabinera*, police woman, always made him come home on time. The stern northerner (of Dutch descent), sturdy and draconian, waited up for him, carpet beater and sharp tongue at the ready. It was her own choice to stay behind in the ivory tower at night, though he was the one who made her wait for his return. The street was too far down to make him out in the crowd. All she saw after he left was a mass of anonymous dots; one of them had to be him, she knew. From down below, words floated up (after the tango by Homero Expósito and Domingo Federico):

THE SORROWS OF CORRIENTES STREET

Street, straight as a stream
cadging cash for crusts of bread

Avenue running through
the city like a vale of dread,
how sad and pale
are all your lights!
Your pillars and signs
sighing bright.
Your billboards
flashing cardboard smiles!
Laughter that comes after
courage found in alcohol.
Sighs, melodic lies
that sell us sweethearts for a song.
Jumble sale of sad delights
where caresses are traded
and illusions thrive.
Miserable? Yes...
because you're ours.
Sad? Yes...
because you dream.
Your joy is sadness
and the pain of waiting
courses through you...
and makes you wither
in the pale light!
Gloomy? Yes...
because you're ours.
Sad? Yes...
you're down and out.
Slobs, whose only job is
posing as bohemians,
amigos with no pesos

just the dream of going far
that keeps them going,
drinking coffee
at a table in some bar.
Street, straight as a stream
cadging cash for crusts of bread
Avenue running through
the city like a vale of dread
where you were sold by men
and betrayed like Christ
and where the Obelisk's dagger
forever bleeds you dry.

He always came home at unpredictable hours, always late at night when she, unable to sleep, would still be waiting. Tossing and turning in the heat, stewing in her loneliness. Locked up in that tower with only the skies for company – surrounded by fantasies, fata morganas, illusions and, far down below, the will-o'-the-wisp lights indicating the places he spent his evenings in the company of so many other women.

Everything happened there, and she was stuck here. Oh, the jealousy! He didn't even try to hide it, came barging in with lipstick smudges still on his cheeks, a different scent at his throat every time, hairs on the shoulders of his disheveled jacket. Still drunk and roguishly cheerful, he would fling his clothes over the back of a chair as she lay in bed watching him. The woman lying on her side like a sculpture, nude and frowning, head resting on one arm. Poor mummy, he thought, dressed in your shroud, lying in your coffin. Do I have to sleep beside to you tonight, in the stuffy tomb you have made of our marital bed?

The next morning, he could hide behind his desk, escape into his consular duties, take refuge in his poems, pop outside for a cup of coffee, until later, in the evening, the evening...

She could do what was expected of a woman on a day like that: there were plenty of windows to clean, as many as twenty-eight of them looking out on all sides of the apartment, and she watched the strings of vinegar water zigzagging across the skies as if savagely crossing out his twilights.

Their record player lamented (after the tango by Carlos César Lenzi and Edgardo Donato):

And everything happens at dusk,
which magically conjures up love,
at twilight comes the first kiss,
at twilight, the two of us...
And everything happens at dusk
like a sunset on the inside.
How velvety soft it is
the dusky half-light of love.

One day, he brought home a girl. Her name was María Luisa Bombal, a young actress with literary aspirations whom they had met back in Santiago, where she had made a suicide attempt after being dumped by her lover. My father and mother, both getting broody, had befriended her with parental tenderness and invited her to stay with them at their Buenos Aires apartment until she got back on her feet. And now she had arrived.

"Look who I've brought along!" he who would be my father shouted delightedly from the hall that morning. "Our new mongoose," and he pushed the young actress ahead of him down the hall toward my mother standing in the kitchen, and she exclaimed excitedly over her shoulder, "María Luisa! She made it!" and still clutching the tea towel, she trotted happily toward the girl and almost smothered her in a somewhat rigid embrace that was meant to express her joy and hospitality with Argentinian vivacity but didn't quite succeed in masking her Nordic bashfulness.

María Luisa beamed when she saw the view of the good skies on all sides, and stepping into the kitchen, said in wide-eyed, delighted amazement, "What a beautiful, large table!"

"All the better for writing on," my future father growled.

"And what a beautiful marble floor," cried María Luisa ecstatically.

"All the better for thinking on. The white marble is veined with grey, like paper covered in handwriting. That corner over there is where I put my manuscripts. Over here at this table leg, the sheets of discarded lines of poetry flutter down when I'm writing, I hope it won't disturb you. You can write as much as you like while you're here. May this environment be an inspiration to you."

"Yes. Yes!" María Luisa exclaimed. It all seemed even more beautiful to her than she had imagined from the novels. "I'm sure it will! It will," she cried girlishly (at thirty-three summers old, she didn't look a day over twenty). I have to admit she was very beautiful, with her symmetrical features, large brown eyes the color of hazelnuts, straight fringe and well-defined eyebrows. My father was already envisaging scenes of nocturnal discussions of their respective work (late at night when my future mother Marietje would be fast asleep) taking place at that table. His hand on her wrist while he whispered advice close to her ear, "You should rewrite that sentence like this, and oh, there's a comma too many over here." On her knee, "Well done, my girl, you're very talented!" But María Luisa, who could spot advances coming centuries beforehand (as she put it in a metaphor that delighted my future father), determined that each should choose their own side of the table, divided by a watershed, and pointing at the flower vase in the middle of the tabletop, said (with mock sternness), there, the flowers marked the dividing line, and my soon-to-be-father shook his head with an equally feigned good-natured laugh at what he saw as that endearing, enraging, child-like cunning of hers.

She outsmarted him at every turn. He was no match for her lightning mind. Finally admitting defeat, he threw his hands up in the air in exasperation, put her on a pedestal, cajoled her along with throw-away remarks over his shoulder to his writer friends, where he introduced her as the only woman he had ever met with whom he could have a serious discussion about literature. María Luisa archly cut short such songs of praise: "You look for mothers in your lovers, but not all of us are suitable for motherhood."

My almost-mother was standing next to her, only glad she was able to understand the Spanish. She took all the compliments paid to her guest in her stride, knowing she couldn't hold a candle to her anyway, that she herself was at a double disadvantage: the cruel, irrevocable lack of both the native language to express herself in and the literary capacity that would have allowed her to do so.

In the evenings, he often went to dinner parties like the ones given by the notorious magazine tycoon and multimillionaire whose library was furnished with leopard, panther and ocelot skins and contained only incunabula. Game on the spit was dished up on a huge table for my future father, his friend Federico and a lady guest, an ethereal poet, who my father claimed had her eyes fixed on him rather than Federico throughout the meal.

By day, he was at the consulate. The two Marías went out together, arm in arm, drinking coffee and shopping, strolling, chatting, looking at hats, feeling fabrics, ogling jewellery they couldn't afford, and to my future mother's surprise, they soon became as close as sisters, bosom friends.

In an atmosphere heavy with desperation and betrayal that

permeated the bars they visited and the living room at home, my mother found the courage to pour her heart out to her new friend, who (given she herself was tortured by a broken heart that had driven her to attempt suicide) was sure to understand.

This – tango line – is how my mother told the story of her husband's coldness – tango line.

Glasses were topped up to steady the nerves. My almost-mother talked. María Luisa nodded. I have only ever seen women use this nod, this motion of the head that simultaneously conveys disgust at what is said and agreement with the speaker and her opinion. I, a posthumous spy on this scene from before I was born, listen to silences like dragging movements that suddenly flagged, at which the other woman nodded, placing her nods like little steps in between the feet of the sudden silence until the first again took up the thread and carried on with stronger steps, and the other followed with a shake of the head, a hiss from the tip of the tongue, disapproving tut-tutting like tip-of-the-toe-tap-tapping and palate-clacking at the back of the mouth like the click of a heel, a rotating leg, accompanying the long strides with which the speaker distanced herself, observing her own emotions from the side.

My mother was the lead, María Luisa followed. The words of the tango lilted in the background.

In the silence afterwards, María Luisa quickly launched into a short monologue, a solo, breaking free from my mother-to-be's story, at arm's length but still in the same vein ("men are such bastards!"), connected by an invisible thread (the tenor), and so María Luisa began her lonely dying swan dance about the lover who had abandoned her, dancing almost to death, but then came my mother's life-saving step in her direction, approaching open-armed, lean on me, the woman whose forehead now almost touched the floor as in another struggle not to succumb to suicide, but thank god: in a single swift movement María Luisa straightened up, at just the right chords (this had only been a feint – years later, she would attempt to shoot him), and they turned, twirled and whirled until my intended father, tired from his work, interrupted this scene I was enjoying so much with his appearance, "Mongoose, are you coming? The literary world awaits," he grinned while already preparing to go out again for the night.

"Maruca, are you coming too?" María Luisa quasi-echoed. My mother went with them, arm in arm and under the wing of María Luisa, who also spoke English and was always nice to her; and the trio bustled to the elevator, looking from above like three shield bugs in admirable formation around a street light that the municipal lighting department had hung in the middle of the road. Three moths around a candle flame that threatened to scorch their wings...

;

They walked down Avenida Corrientes, and hitting the running road in María Luisa's company, the woman on the verge of becoming my mother felt light and happy. I can see the glow radiating from her, a halo of lightness, and for a short moment feel relieved as well.

They walked past doors swinging open now and then to fling strings of music out into the street, navigated around groups of dawdlers moving so slowly they seemed to be holding meetings in the middle of the road, unlinked their arms for a moment to let people through who were walking the other way. And so the two Marías, accompanied by my father, arrived at the building of the Argentinian PEN Club, where they were introduced to the legendary Spanish poet Federico García Lorca, and where my father and Lorca later held the following speech:

My father-to-be: "Ladies …"

Lorca: "… and gentlemen. In bullfighting, there is something called the *toreo del alimón*, in which two toreros dodge the bull together by holding one cape between them."

My father: "Federico and I, connected by an electric wire, will now face the critical challenge of this very impressive reception together."

Lorca: "It is customary at such gatherings for poets, silver-tongued or wooden, to improvise a speech in their own, living words, as a salute to their colleagues and friends."

My father: "We, however, are going to welcome a dead guest into your midst, an abandoned widower, shrouded in the shadow of a greater death than is granted to others, widowed by Life, whose brilliant spouse he was in his heyday; standing in the fiery shadow of his wings, we will repeat his name until his wizardry rises from oblivion."

Lorca: "After sending our embraces, gentle as penguins, to our sensitive poet Amado Villar, we will now, in the certainty that wine glasses will be smashed, forks leap up seeking the eyes they long for and a tidal wave will stain the damask, fling a great name onto the tabletop. We give you the name of America and Spain's foremost poet: Rubén …"

My father: "Darío. For, ladies …"

Lorca: "… and gentlemen,"

My father: "where in Buenos Aires is the Rubén Darío Square?"

Lorca: "Where is the statue of Rubén Darío?"

My father: "He loved parks. Where is the Rubén Darío Park?"

Lorca: "Where the Rubén Darío flower shop?"

My father: "Where the Rubén Darío apple tree, and where the Rubén Darío apples?"

Lorca: "Where is Rubén Darío's severed hand?"

My father: "Where, indeed?"

Lorca: "Rubén Darío was laid to rest in his ancestral Nicaragua, underneath a hideous plaster lion, of the kind that grace the gates of rich people's houses."

My father: "A mock lion for the founder of lions, a lion with no stars for a man who dedicated the stars to others."

Lorca: "He captured the sound of the jungle in a single adjective, like Friar Luis de Granada – master of languages – he created constellations out of the lemon and the deer's hoof and the molluscs full of terror and infinity; he sent us out to sea with ships and shadows reflected in our pupils and he constructed an alley of gin across the greyest evening the sky had ever known and greeted the south-westerly wind as an equal, chest out, like a romantic poet, placing his hand on the Corinthian capital, wistfully and ironically skeptical of all ages."

My father: "His red name is worthy of being remembered in all its essential dimensions, together with his terrible heartaches, his incandescent uncertainty, his descent to the circles of hell, his ascent to the castles of fame, his attributes of a great poet, indispensable from the first moment until the end of time."

Lorca: "As a Spanish poet, he taught Spanish children and their teachers, with a sense of universality and generosity which today's poets so sorely lack. He taught Valle-Inclán and Juan Ramón Jiménez, as well as the Machado brothers, and his voice was water and saltpetre in the furrows of our venerable Mother Tongue. From Rodrigo Caro to the Argensola brothers and don Juan Arguijo, the Spanish language never knew such a feast of words, such collisions of consonants, lights and forms as in Rubén Darío. From Velázquez' landscapes to Goya's pyre, and from Quevedo's melancholy to the cult of apple-cheeked Majorcan peasant girls, Darío walked Spain's soil as if it were his own land."

My father: "A spring tide, the warm sea of the North brought him to Chile, where the waves left him behind, alone on the rocky, jagged coast where the ocean whipped him with froth and flakes and the black wind of Valparaíso covered him with singing salt. Let us erect a statue to him tonight from the air that is permeated with smoke and voice, and with circumstances and with life, just like his magnificent poetic work is permeated with dreams and sounds."

Lorca: "But on this statue of air, I want to lay his blood like a wreath of corals swayed by the surf, his nerves like the photograph of branched lightning, his Minotaur head on which the Gongoresque snow has been sketched by a flight of hummingbirds, his vague, absent eyes of a teardrop millionaire, but also his failings: the weed-infested, worm-eaten bookshelves with the voice of a hollow flute, the brandy bottles of his dramatic delirium, his endearingly bad taste and his shamelessly shallow phrases that make the greater part of his verse so human. Defying all norms, forms and schools, the seminal power of his poetry has endured."

This went on for twenty minutes, until my father and Lorca finally concluded their duologue with the following words:

My father: "Federico García Lorca, Spaniard, and I, Chilean, the two of us are passing responsibility for this evening among friends to each other, and to the great shadow whose song was more elevated than ours and who greeted the Argentinian soil we tread with a voice unlike any ever heard on it before."

Lorca: "Pablo Neruda, Chilean, and I, Spaniard, are united by our language and by the great Nicaraguan poet who was also Argentinian, Chilean and Spanish: Rubén Darío."

My father and Lorca: "In whose honor and glory we raise our glasses."

EIGHT

JUST IMAGINE: THIS SHARD of my father's life reached me, high on my hereafter raft, just as I was returning to the state of being unborn, among the clinking of raised glasses and the buzz of voices of the living, those present at that moment, in that place. It sang its way through to the pre-uterine me, like an underwater sound, muffled, tempered by the absence of time, and I wasn't even able to use Oskar's magic drumsticks to summon the knowledge of the unknown past, as they would have drowned out the buzzing and clinking too much. With only the ears of one already dead, an as-yet-unborn, an imminent emergent, I heard. I seemed to be listening in from another room, like a visitor staying the night or a child that is supposed to be asleep but has actually tip-toed to the top of the stairwell of time, and there I crouched, eavesdropping, and, peering through a crack in the door of mortality, I saw everything that happened that night.

And still I observe all in the dissonance of my absence, in the primal scream of my nonbeing, through the void of my breath and the opiate of my voice. The rising water of my hydrocephalic skull washes away everything, into the gaping hole my absence has gouged into my future father and mother's life, and this is where I bellow out my despair and no one hears me, not one of the people seated at the long table, those obsessed with the late Rubén Darío, with Lorca

57

and with my father. I could have lived in their pores, in their crumbs, in their farts if necessary, but was denied even that by my father, the great maker of names, the great dropper of names and the great concealer of my humble name. I screech and scream in complete silence, the silence of the grave, of obscurity, of concealment. I moan and rage for nothing and no one. Do you hear me, Hagar: I moan and rage, I tell you, for nothing and for no one!

There, during the verbal bullfight from which my father and Lorca emerged more or less as equals, I was conceived by a primal spark that shot from his flood of words and leapt to my mother, who couldn't make head or tail of what was being said and almost nodded off in the darkness of the audience while Lorca was ogling my father, wooing him with words (which no one noticed as he concealed his forbidden love), having finally found his great soulmate (when Federico was executed by fascists, my father married his body of thought because he couldn't marry the man himself; he became a Communist, and always stated Federico's execution as the reason).

And Federico: I saw him in all his desperation, his passion, his love for my father. Only I understood it, a fellow reject of my father's.

Federico García Lorca, recently arrived in Buenos Aires for the premiere of his play *Blood Wedding*, was already a sensation, a true legend, and so as not to damage this popularity he decided it would be best to keep his homosexuality a secret, though he did confide in my father.

If only my father and Lorca's courtship song had planted the seed for my birth. I'm telling you, Hagar, it would have been better than the biologically more likely union that did bring me into being.

But alas, my father was touched by the fire of Buenos Aires! It made him wild, eager, drunk on triumph. He took it out on my mother that evening, a night of falsehood, in which he poked up a fire in her that set her ablaze.

After the overwhelming success of his speech, my future father threw himself at my future mother as if pouncing on himself, or as if charging at that rag of language with which he and Lorca had baffled the bull of rhetoric, the words spoken that evening still ringing in his mind. Turned on by himself, he slaked his lust making love to himself on top of her, full to overflowing of himself until she, too, was filled with him.

Oskar, the meddling pest, is about to interfere. I can tell from the deadpan expression on his midget's face. And drowning out my words with his drumbeat, he starts to speak. Rattling off his version of my tale, the way he thinks I should tell it:

"Somewhere on his long journey across the horizon, on one of his trips in the orient, my father managed to get hold of a copy of the Kamasutra, or perhaps it had been a gift to him as a consul. In any case, the book was far too difficult for the ill-fated couple who would be my parents, and they soon tossed it aside in irritation, dismissing the positions as unsuitable for their clumsy bodies. Even the book's covers on the floor were sprawled at an angle eighty-five degrees wider than their legs were capable of spreading, and so they resigned to doing it their own way, using the long-established positions which I, in my role of child and the fruit of such whims, do not wish to know in detail and therefore refuse to even visualize, resulting in the absence of certain passages that, though they would have boosted the sales of this work no end, would harm my integrity as offspring – in short, I'm not telling, and that's final!

"I won't even mention the names my father the poet invented for the poses they performed; oh, all right then, just the one: 'prick pirouette,' which is surely capable of tickling only the funny bone, especially with hindsight, in view of their flesh-and-blood legacy."

Oskar shows no sign of stopping. He keeps up his pesky

drumming, putting these words into my mouth: "I can trace the exact journey I made from the discarding of the book and my parents' groaning through to my own origin – I remember a handful of black grit, the stars tilting, a big bang that was ear-splitting only to myself, Mercury lurching into a trajectory to chase Pluto out of the seventh house in which cats' eyes fixed me with adoring looks from every window and there was a moon so full and bright it made me queasy; a train derailing, a clock striking seven, birdsong, a cartload of indistinct objects – produce of some sort – and somewhere between the moon in the eighth house and my mother's sighing insides I must have been conceived, and immediately afterwards, the moon still in the eighth house but the sun and Saturn in the fourth, while The Lovers appeared next to The Hanged Man, Tower and Devil flanked The Chariot and Strength stood on its head, Destiny struck."

One afternoon, sheltered by the protective atmosphere of eternity, in the quivering light of an autumn sun and the ever-rising spring moons and accompanied by hours of drumrolls and sighing of tinsel and heartbeams, Oskar cooked up the story of his own conception, even more dominated by omens and augury than my father and mother's meeting. I still find my parents' union hard to accept, exactly because its taking place was so completely unnecessary.

By beating on his tin drum, Oskar can recall everything about events he could not possibly have witnessed himself. He has leant me his drumsticks so I can try it for myself. I only make reluctant use of them, and only on the rare occasions my own posthumous all-knowingness fails me unexpectedly, as they come with a major drawback: they plunge everything into an Oskar Matzerathian haze which my Malvian gaze can only penetrate with the greatest difficulty, and they kindle a rebelliousness and defiance in me I would never have thought myself capable of. On earth, my midget friend used his voice, accompanied by drumrolls, to shatter glass and cause upheaval whenever he didn't like what was going on around him (the wooden drumsticks like extensions of his father's moralistically wagging finger, just as Pinocchio's wooden nose was a physical extension of his lies).

I don't believe Oskar's version of events. It must definitely have been a word spark that shot over the heads of the other guests that evening, guided unerringly toward my mother by her overripe receptiveness, where it penetrated her body through goodness knows which orifice, and germinated. In this nocturnal spark that broke free of my father and catapulted itself to my mother lay the seed of my future inadequate self.

;

Nausea. The surge of an inner sea. Waves beating in her belly. Rolling and dying down. She retched, threw up a seaweedy substance. Lurching all over the skyscraper's twentieth floor as if on deck of a storm-tossed ship, heavy, heaving, fearing the tower block would tip over, that she would fall on the city down below, flatten it with her pregnancy: from November 1933, my mother was pregnant in Buenos Aires.

This was the base for my burgeoning birth and the soil for my breath: the death they wrote; the father, the lady friend, the tango composers and their poet pal. Death was on all of their lips. For while I was growing in my mother's belly, becoming more and more complete, Federico attended the opening night of his gory *Blood Wedding*, in which almost all the characters butcher each other, María Luisa wrote *The Shrouded Woman*, and my father wrought his most sinister poems, including "Widower's Tango" to the former mistress he still pined for, Josie Bliss. María Luisa created a novel while I was created inside my mother, simultaneously, line for line, cell division for cell division; twin Marías. And in the meantime, at the same table where María Luisa wrote *The Final Mist* and *The Shrouded Woman*, my father finished the second part of his *Residence on Earth*.

But I! I! I would have become his greatest hurdle on this earth, that is beyond a doubt; I was the stagnation, the stumbling block, the setback that would have kept him from everything else in his life. If he had stayed with me, he could no longer have been anywhere else. But I'm getting ahead of myself. I've long since come to understand why my father would later burn his bridges. It was either me or an entire continent at his feet. With his back to me and his face to the world, there was nothing he couldn't do. But what am I babbling about? Of course it was never a conscious choice.

At the time, my mother still enjoyed listening to the delicate sound of the two pens at the kitchen table; how softly they scratched, and how deeply they cut. The simpleton was grateful to have another soul in the apartment, and while María Luisa's story about the living dead woman on the bier grew, death was growing along with it in my mother's belly as I was coming to life; a strange concurrence of a living death in a dead person, and a death coming to life in my mother's womb.

The strange gurgling sounds coming from the table in their apartment as the two writers read each other's stories and poems kept my mother going, and beaming. While they gave themselves over to death, she, serene and simple-minded, swelled up with life, blooming, ballooning, bosomy, rosy and round. Ignorant as yet of that life's defects. A full-blown flower, alone on her stalk among dung and garbage, swaying above an abyss of cocaine, whores and whoremongers. Meanwhile, I was gently rocked in her waters; the precursor of that other, that endless flow of water to my brain.

If their days were dominated by death in their writing, the nights were dedicated to the dance of the living. There they went, the lord and lady of the dark, the bat-winged villains in their black capes, flitting along the frayed fringes of tango music, brushing with death, brushing against life, fluttering around a lamp post. Disappearing into the elevator that took them down from their citadel high above the earth and its suffering, high above the poverty and pain down below, they descended twenty floors in the luxurious elevator shaft to take part in the night life on street level, though always at an appropriate distance.

Let those restless spirits roam the night, she thought, let them dance their exhausting rounds of the bars and to oblivion, let them hunt, if that's what they must do. She didn't need to hunt. She was already carrying everything within her. All that mattered to her now was there, inside of her. It allowed her to reconcile herself to her loneliness, her inability to take part in my father's life. Now, the salons that rhythmically blazed through her solitude no longer bothered her.

But time and eternity and the good skies of Buenos Aires lie between my words, your pen and her ears, which were deaf to my misery. She didn't know that decay had already entered deep into her body; that there was no escaping the degeneration growing inside of her. While she had become her own citadel, a tower within a tower, I was nibbling away at her insides, a stowaway, a Trojan horse.

Oskar is egging me on with his drumrolls, so I give in, take the sticks from him and start drumming, and yes, go ahead, write it down: they used cocaine, like all Buenos Aires intellectuals at the time. Including my mother, already pregnant with me.

Now buzz off, Oskar! I suffered a brain hemorrhage during my difficult birth.

Is that the origin of my abnormality, or should I go even further back; is it concealed in the dark forests of Chile? And to the drumming of Oskar's sticks, I dig ever deeper.

NINE

I'D LIKE TO INTRODUCE YOU properly to all the others up here, the people I see every day. It's important you get an idea of my day-to-day afterlife and who exactly I spend it with. There's never a dull moment with them around! I made sure of that by carefully selecting my company: yes, this handful of souls are the only ones capable of continuously diverting, healing and inspiring me.

Look, there's the friendly, full-flushed face of good old Daniel Miller. Watch him tuck into his wedding cake, his funeral sandwich! We get all the left-overs from earth, which is more than enough. Crumbs dangle from his chin.

Turning his face to me, lower jaw still covered in morsels of cake and mouth stuffed full, Daniel makes me the same reproach I told you about earlier in this story: that writing this account is just a way of posthumously getting into my father's good books, that that's the reason I'm going to all this trouble, boring you with the details and making you write them down for me! Daniel calls it a wasted effort, and even if it isn't: pearls before swine. He says there's a reason it's called eternal rest, and that my hard work is disturbing it.

Lucia interrupts him; she disagrees, sticks up for me, and playfully pelting him with chunks and lumps of our food, encourages me to do what I think best, just as she did herself. She has finally found her biographer on earth! In Lucia Joyce's biography, which she claims to have whispered into the author's ear line for line ("I have pulled myself from death by my own hair"), she's been transformed from the dancer she was on earth into a genius; a true artist on the verge of eclipsing her father.

Of course, Daniel Miller doesn't believe a word of it. "Vanitas, vanity in every sense of the word." It's because he has been trying to forget his father, just as his father forgot him. "But tell us again," Oskar, Lucia and I encourage him now, "of your famous father."

;

"Oh, but you've heard it all before," he launches into the story with his usual splutter, "it was in *Vanity Fair* and almost all the papers. I quote by heart. The headline read: Arthur Miller's Missing Act. My father Arthur Miller, in life a famous American playwright and the former husband of Marilyn Monroe, kept my existence a secret for almost four decades because I was born with Down syndrome. Well, can you blame him: one day you have Monroe, the next you have me. But it came to light eventually."

He drops his gaze, lifts it. Continues, "My father, who explored questions of guilt and morality in his writing, all but cut me out of his life after taking me to an institute for the disabled when I was one week old. I, the secret son, suffering from Down syndrome but endowed with other characteristics besides, am not mentioned a single time in my father's memoirs, *Timebends: A Life*. But my father, author of *Death of a Salesman* and *The Crucible*, softened with age. Just six weeks before he gave up the ghost, he added me to his will, leaving me and his normal children an equal share of his estate."

"Amazing what an Oscar can do!" Oskar sneers. "Because it's true, isn't it, that you're the younger brother of Rebecca Miller, the successful and celebrated actress on earth and the widely envied wife of Daniel Day-Lewis? Day-Lewis, who won an Oscar for his role as a handicapped man in *My Left Foot,* is reported to have been 'shocked' at the way his brother-in-law was treated, and perhaps he pressed his father-in-law (possibly to make his own role more plausible) to make amends just before his death."

Daniel nods. "My mother Inge Morath was my father's third wife. She was a photographer, they met when she was taking pictures of Monroe on the set of *The Misfits.* In 1966, she gave birth to me. My father called me a 'mongol.'"

"I prefer semicolon!" I joke.

"Shut up, Malvie," Daniel says with a friendly glance. "My father told a friend that he would hide me, the baby, away. My mother wanted to keep me, but my father refused because he didn't want Rebecca growing up with me – as if he thought I would taint her, the way apples lying close together in a basket will infect each other with rot. I lived there among other equally maggoty minds until I was seventeen, in an overcrowded Connecticut institution that in the eighties was taken to court over its poor living conditions. But despite my handicap, I managed to wriggle out of the institute's grasp and take part in the Special Olympics. I competed in skiing, cycling, athletics and bowling."

We can see his motor system echo the movements of kicking and running feet, carefully aiming fingers and throwing arms. We recognize the glint in his eyes. "I was living with an elderly couple at the time. My sister Rebecca made a point of solemnly calling me 'an important member of the family.' After my father's death, she told journalists writing an article about us that I led a very active, happy life, surrounded by people who loved me. But my father lived in denial. He hardly ever mentioned me to friends and rarely accompanied my mother on her weekly visits to me. 'Miller excised a central character who didn't fit the plot of his life as he wanted it,' journalists wrote when his concealment of my existence came to light after forty years. They declared that their discovery was at odds with my father's reputation of advocate of the downtrodden and left-wing hero while they themselves, the cowards, had waited until my father's death to reveal it."

"Wasn't your father also praised for refusing to give the names of people who sympathized with Communism during the American anti-Communist witch-hunt of the fifties, and for his outspoken protest against the Vietnam war?" Lucia asks.

"In the days following his death, he was celebrated the world over," Daniel nods, not without pride. "The *New York Times* lauded his strong belief that 'man is responsible for his and for his neighbor's actions' and his good friend and colleague, the American playwright Edward Albee, said that my father had held up a mirror to society. Now the mirror had tilted and was suddenly facing him, but the image he'd have seen if he'd had the courage to look, would not have been of his own face but mine!"

Daniel roars with laughter and we roar with him. Oskar gives his drum three jovial whacks. Then Daniel goes on, "The experts say my father wrote his best plays before I was born. They now suggest that 'Miller's guilt,' as my father's behavior toward me is called, may have cast a shadow on his later career. The papers also wrote that my existence was an open secret in my father's circle of friends. 'Whether he was motivated by shame, selfishness, or fear—or, more likely, all three—Miller's failure to tackle the truth created a hole in the heart of his story,' one of the journalists wrote, and, 'One wonders if, in his relationship with Daniel, Miller was sitting on his greatest unwritten play.'" Daniel is quoting by heart, and we all nod our approval. "My existence was first disclosed in a 2003 biography by the American theatre critic Martin Gottfried, who personally did not believe it would damage my father's reputation as a 'great, great playwright.' And this," he says, taking a huge bite out of his wedding cake, "has remained the state of affairs concerning my father's reception of me."

"Not for long now, Daniel, not for long," I console him, and in a posh voice, I mimic the announcement of our play:

"Today, we in the Afterlife are finally the first to present:

DANIEL, THE MISFITS PART II
BY ARTHUR MILLER, POST MORTEM.
THE PLAY HE NEVER WROTE
ON EARTH.

STARRING:
DANIEL MILLER, OSKAR MATZERATH,
MALVA MARINA REYES ALIAS NERUDA
AND LUCIA JOYCE."

Daniel laughs. Quick on the draw, he adds, "It contains a powerful scene in which Arthur is literally groveling in the dust: you can see his kneeling silhouette crawl through an enormous pile of sand, begging our forgiveness, while throwing dramatic shadows on the back screen. Let's sing the song that comes afterward again."

And we burst into song, in our archangel castrati voices:

"Oh yes! Oh yes! They need us, the bows made of bones
the kids with hydrocephalic heads the size of the sun
the Cyclops-eyed, the Siamese twins

or those with multiple muzzles, tripple-fork-toed feet,
ossified skin and brittled bones

stunted arms and legs, missing fingers and toes

the legacy's whole menagerie
that parade of mutants, goose-stepping off the mortal coil
with genes wildly out of line, driven

> *amok*

> **amok**   driven amok!

> amok

> amok

As new technologies, genetic sampling
embryo selection, cloning
maneuver and manipulation
have almost cut off the path to us

have already almost cut- have cut us-
off!"

Oskar is frantically accompanying us on his drum. Lucia and I dance
a tango in the background like wayang shadow puppets.

TEN

THE WORDS OF OUR SONG have barely died down when we hear, from very close, the sound of two clapping hands. Socrates, wakened by our mention of his name earlier in this saga, has joined us at our table. Incidentally, he himself left behind a wife and three children when he drank the cup of poison at the age of seventy. He looks out at us from his large, bald skull, fixing us with the dazzling, horny satyr gaze he was so famous for, as ugly as the statues of Silenus which the young Alcibiades compared him with. He's got one of those little statues with him and places it clumsily on Daniel's lap, who turns it around in his hands and notices it opens up like a Russian doll to reveal another figure inside.

"It's an idol! A beautiful idol!" Socrates is wheezing into Daniel's ear. "That is what you and I have in common with each other, and with the ugly statues of Silenus: hideous on the outside but pure gold on the inside, that's us! By the way, Lucia, when will you finally come around to introducing me to Stephen Dedalus?"

Without waiting for Lucia's reply, he takes the statue out of the midget drummer's hands which the latter had been examining attentively.

Encouraged by the old Athenian's words, Oskar gets up and starts to parade around our table like a manic soldier, then goes over to the other tables and recites his part of the score in an uninterrupted stream. Puffing out his pigeon chest, he marches across the smooth, grey-veined marble of the dining hall floor, bending toward a table occasionally, addressing his audience on either side. His drumsticks tucked under his arms. The rest of us stand up and take a bow.

Then the curtain falls.

ELEVEN

THE SINGING AND SILLINESS flooding the room from our table appears to have reached the adjacent dining rooms too.

"We, the dead," Goethe says, sighing heavily as he stands at our table and leans over Daniel, "need to pass the time somehow." The venerable old man explains his belief that the only bonds shackling us together after death are the friendships we choose ourselves, based on elective affinities, instead of the suffocating blood ties that so often made life on earth a misery.

"Taken together, blood and kinship are a dismal thing." Goethe considers himself lucky, he says, that on his arrival up here, all blood ties and the accompanying duties, burdens and debts were finally abolished. (Could that be why I can't find my father here?) To him, it is the greatest boon of the afterlife, and he wonders what gave us the idea that Arthur Miller would feel compelled to write a play about Daniel, the disabled son he rejected on earth, given that all such relationships are canceled after death.

We're forced to admit that the play is a wishful dream, evoked by Oskar's drumming. We tell him we were so keen to finally take the limelight that we wrote the scenario ourselves and currently perform it every evening, purely for our own and each other's entertainment.

Oh, but he does understand, the old man adds sweetly; and nodding his approval, Goethe shuffles back to his seat.

Meanwhile, I still can't take my eyes off Lucia. As she wearily runs her fingers through her hair, I see her entire earthly life stretch out behind her; I can look straight through her, past her slender shoulder blades and down the path of her life, into the big wide world of the past. And there, along the way, I spot the figures of her father, her mother, her brother, her schoolmistress; I can see the complete pandemonium of earthlings acting out the pantomime of her life while trampling the genius underfoot.

There is the chair again, the one Lucia flung at her mother's head in desperation, at the cold-hearted, jealous serpent who had never heard of puberty before and would not hear of it then, and again I watch the scene of her unjustified confinement in the mental institution.

But then I'm suddenly distracted by a painful dig in the ribs: Oskar, the career midget, is elbowing me. He's the smallest of the four of us, much shorter even than me. His head only just peeks over the edge of the table, even though he's sitting on his tin drum that he placed on his chair for extra height. His wooden drumsticks lie next to the cutlery on the right side of his plate.

"What is it?" I ask because of the dig, but instead of an answer he gives me such a saucy wink that I'm full up for the rest of the evening.

;

After the meal, we go horseback riding. Every evening after dinner, Oskar, Daniel, Lucia and I like to canter and career across a different stretch of the eternal plains of the afterlife. Lucia's thoroughbred stallion is going at a modest trot, while the rest of us gallop along on our pony (Daniel), miniature donkey (Oskar) and miniature horse (me). If you listen very carefully, you might just hear our voices – thin, high-pitched screams filtering through the low-hanging branches we ride underneath and echoing over the wide fields. We are thoroughly enjoying ourselves, throwing our voices like lassoes, fully aware we are inverted Don Quixotes and Sancho Panzas; in our case, the windmills are real and we ourselves are the ghosts.

At my old friend Johann Wolfgang von Goethe's house, I call a quick break. Climbing down from my docile little horse, I can see my old friend is home and enter the cottage without knocking. I find him seated at the table, holding a flower in his hands.

"Look, Malva," he says softly without raising his eyes. His back has already seen me. "*Sidalcea malviflora.* She enables me to carry on the research I began on earth. There is nothing I take more pride in than my scientific work; none of my literary masterpieces mean half as much to me. I tried to fuse science and poetry into an actual symbiosis, and succeeded in *The Metamorphosis of Plants.* My research even inspired Darwin to develop his theory of evolution. For haven't I proved that a plant in its entirety is actually nothing more than a unfurling leaf? Doesn't the growth and development of the plant already contain its completion, the goal that lies dormant within it and unfolds itself as it grows? Isn't the petal, the pistil, the stem – everything about the plant – actually metamorphosed leaf, developed into its final form of petal, pistil, root, stem, et cetera? Thus the spirit of the future plant is already incorporated in its seed, which only needs to mature to achieve that archetypal form, its core essence. Is this archetypal form not common to all plants? Is that not why they resemble each other so much, because they all evolved from the same basis, the same primordial form?"

"Yes, Malva," he continues in a different, gentler voice. "I know what you're thinking, what you're wondering, now: how come this completion did not happen in your case, even though you, as a human being, also contained such a primal form which needed only to unfurl itself as you developed and lo and behold, there you'd have been: a normal and beautiful girl! A healthy, lovely child. I know, but sometimes unexpected interventions, blockades, occur, caused by unforeseen external circumstances. This can happen just as easily in the course of the development of one organism as in that of a generation, a family, or a nation. Alas, it evidently cannot always be prevented. Though the primeval form already contains health as its final goal, you can never be sure of actually reaching it. But let this comfort you, dear child. Let the sight of me holding this small, infinitely fragile flower between my fingers be a consolation to you; look at me, hunched over the petals day after day, working tirelessly to understand everything about this plant. Science is advancing, has advanced. However much we may despair in the face of ever-recurring diseases, war and injustice, the progress of science, understanding and healing have always marched on alongside them. In your time on earth, there was no cure yet for a deformity like yours, but thanks to science, thanks to the diligent research and meticulous work of scientists, many patients with the same form of hydrocephalus you suffered and died from can now be successfully treated."

Moving closer, I see five mauve petals like tiny splayed digits reaching out as if grasping at happiness, and he lets me feel and stroke them while he mutters softly, "When I discovered, back on earth, that every part of the plant repeats its archetypal form in exactly the same proportions, I was holding just such a flower," and his fingers point and I see it and I thank him and go back to my pony because the others are waiting. My horse greets me with a delighted whinny and rubs its manes against my cheeks. The fields and sun-drenched plains glow invitingly.

TWELVE

WHEN OSKAR BEATS HIS DRUM, he makes a wormhole in the universe. His drumming opens up other dimensions, like the shamanic dance of the caveman, the troglodyte, the exorcist. Through the dusk and dusty light of time opening like a curtain, the fields of eternity and of the past stretch out before us again, and accompanied by drumrolls we mount our horse, pony, mini horse and mini donkey and trot over the endless plains, and there, in the distance, I spot your father again.

;

Equipped with hats, lassoes and gaucho belts, your father and his friend ride across the railway track and turn right into the dried-up river bed. It is a day in July 1970. That morning they had slept in before finally going on this long-planned Riding Trip. They went to a *finca* in the village where they caught and saddled their own horses. What a chatterbox that future father of yours is, forever nattering with everyone he meets. His jabbering silhouette is in constant motion, and whenever he discusses anything of interest with one of his countless conversation partners, he diligently writes it down in his diary (on the cover of the Argentinian notebook there are two small figures on which he has drawn glasses, beards, mustaches and holsters with pistols in them).

Significantly, his first sentence reads:

"In Latin America, people talk a lot."

Well, of course. He does!

And he babbles on, continuing, "In my estimation, the average inhabitant here generates between one and a half and twice as many words daily as the typical Dutch citizen. And all over the continent, this surplus is devoted to football. Except in Chile. Here, it feeds into a very different passion: politics."

Throughout his trip, he published articles on Latin America. He described the revolution from the perspective of that part of the world. The gist of one of those stories: "Despite the over one thousand revolts, coups and revolutions over the past one hundred and fifty years, nothing has changed in Latin America. Hunger and oppression, corruption and serfdom, terror and exploitation are as rampant as ever." He experienced some of that oppression first-hand on the day he was arrested in the Bolivian mining town Oruro without warning or charges brought against him, and kept in custody for almost three weeks. Probable motive: suspicion of contact with guerrilla fighters.

In Amsterdam, meanwhile, your future mother saw him in the paper wearing the jumper she had knit for him, lit candles and vowed to be faithful to her very own Che Guevara.

But at this moment he is still only halfway through the journey which – as he himself does not yet know – is set to come to such an unfortunate end in a couple of months and to start afresh with a tragedy several years later.

He writes, sitting on a rock in the scorching sun with his shirt buttoned open and knees apart, while the Chileans declare him insane and the women slow their pace to stare. And this image, thrown into stark relief by the sunlight flooding over that stone, has been preserved for me to describe to you.

THIRTEEN

BEFORE MY INFIRMITY WAS DISCOVERED (in the sweet phase of ignorance, the tree of knowledge still untouched), there was the song of the blood, the rumba beat of the pulse, the rushing and seething that blended into a peaceful, monotonous hum coming from somewhere in the open space I suspected all around me. Slumbering in the umber darkness of my mother's belly, cradled by her rolling waters like a boat on the swell, I was asleep, awake and in all the stages in between.

An almighty tug put an end to the blissful rocking and swaying that could have gone on forever if it had been up to me, and which even the most beautiful afterlife can't measure up to. Like a car crash in mid-birth, I came to a sudden halt, blocked, stuck, somewhere halfway between life in and out of the womb, in a pitch black tunnel. I had to be pulled into the light of day by force.

The orifice was too tight for my head. Not surprising given the size it had already reached, though its rampant, unstoppable growth had not even started yet. Nevertheless, I was eventually squeezed out, into a cool hospital room from which the scorching Madrid heat of August 18, 1934, had been shut out very effectively. We did all we could, my mother, the doctors and me; and Nature, who took over with a power that is an exclusive preserve of hers.

And so it went on: I clambered out of the moist insides, the light of life flashed through me and the cold fire of the outside world unfurled my hands. Their salving breath on my eyes. There was the heavenly dew, the thirsting for the sweet milk of my mother's breast, there were vague outlines of first things, as yet nameless to me. (This is how my father might have described it if I hadn't turned out to be misshapen. But don't worry, these aren't my father's words. They are my very own!) And that is how, here in Madrid where my father had been offered his next consular post after Buenos Aires and Barcelona, I slid down an endless chute and was dropped slam-bang into my body and into a life that, to this day, I consider my Personal Ice Age.

Then the shrill, shrieking words rang out, wiping out nine months of hope:

"Malva Marina."

The nurse read out the name on the card above my head with a pinched voice. Malva Marina Trinidad del Carmen Reyes Basoalto. As if reciting a prayer. She fiddled nervously with the sheet containing the records, the data, the charts, the numbers, the figures, the calculations, the curves, the abnormalities, the prognoses, the medical conditions, the anxieties; then pulled herself together and smiled.

She had recognized me.

Once a mutant, always a mutant. She crossed herself, the crucifix dangling over her cleavage in the starched white uniform swaying to and fro.

My father (still ignorant of my true form) nodded with satisfaction. It was what he had called me. He named me after a flower, a coastal plant. Malva Marina. Malva, the mallow; a simple plant, charming in its plainness. A flower with no pretensions. Modeling me from small petals, he called me by my name. A last attempt to bring poetry into my life, it was actually a stable door after a bolted horse, a pearl before swine, for after my birth that name soon became meaningless, eclipsed by my head, which from the first moment started pushing everything else aside.

More doctors appeared at my bedside. They saw my head, and the next thing I was the girl with hydrocephalus, water on the brain. I became a case – a rare case, admittedly, though one that had been seen before. From that moment on, I would belong to the species of the *hydrocephali*; a group whose characteristics canceled out any uniqueness my existence may have had.

Mutants, that's what we were. Pitiful monstrosities produced by Nature's abundant diversity. The surplus of her over-abundance. Given this profusion, small errors are inevitable: some of us had three legs, others two arms ending in paws, or stunted limbs – too much of this, too little of that, there was always something wrong.

The doctors bent lower over me. They soon observed it wouldn't be easy to keep me alive, to fit me into the simple harness of growth, feeding and development. My stubborn, obstinate head, my unruly skull, was the problem. With complete calm and enviable control, they shook their own perfectly formed heads, as if not really taking my failure to heart. At this point, my father was still upset by the news, worried, standing at my cradle. Watching over me in long hollow evenings, he wrote a couple of poems: "Illnesses in My Home" and "Maternity." They were long-winded lamentations. His dedication touches me now. If only my head could have been kept in check as easily as his handwriting on the lined paper that prevented any overly erratic strokes of the pen.

There were moments of great danger in which my parents, thinking I would die, didn't know which way to turn. My father paced the corridors, wringing his hands, eyes bloodshot with worry and lack of sleep.

They spent sleepless nights and days, he writing feverish letters to anyone who would listen about my birth and how much he suffered from having to go to the shops (while she was still confined to bed, with me) for all kinds of gruesome orthopaedic devices, measuring cups, funnels and pipettes.

To his horror, nourishment had to be forced on me through a feeding tube. They stuck syringes with serum into my oral cavity and tried to let milk flow in through my lips with a small spoon, but I kept spitting out the disgusting stuff, pressing my petal-shaped lips together stubbornly and turning away my head, which had gone purple, with a dexterousness that seemed to refute even the smallest suggestion of disability.

All of this was much to the dismay of the nursing staff – in those days completely powerless against my condition – and later, at home, of my father. That said, he almost immediately left the fussing with pipettes, syringes, nappies and teaspoons to my mother, as he believed that pipettes and syringes were ultimately just nipple substitutes and as such belonged as firmly to the category of "domestic objects for women's use" as pots and pans, cutlery and crockery, and my mother agreed to everything just as long as I stayed alive.

Too squeamish to clip his own nails, he wouldn't dream of putting his child's chances of survival at risk by messing about with the paraphernalia needed for feeding it; had she forgotten how clumsy he was? All his skills were bunched together in his fist as long as it held a pen, but the moment he opened his hand, everything he touched turned to mud, and she knew that. She wouldn't want him ruining everything with his clumsiness. And so, and because she was plagued by a strange, misplaced feeling of guilt, she said, "Here, I'll do it."

In a letter he wrote to my grandfather a week after my difficult birth – my head, to the kindly observer, still seemed just about proportionate in size – my father called me "the girl." Of course my battle for survival was not over yet, he wrote, but he believed it was almost won and that I would soon grow strong and plump.

He wrote that I was very small, weighing just under 2.5 kilos at birth, but that I was very beautiful. Yup, that's what he wrote to my grandfather, and not a word about my hydrocephalus. I didn't understand either at first – when I set eyes on these words after my death, I had to read them at least four times before I was able to grasp what they actually said. My father had really written to my grandfather that I was as beautiful as a little doll, that I had blue eyes like my grampa, that fortunately I had my mother's nose but that I had his mouth.

I walked on air that whole day; in all my ghostly life I have never felt that light again. I swam with the clouds the way other people swim with dolphins and attributed the same blind benevolence to the whole cosmos, for the difference between myself and nature had vanished now that, at least once in my life, my presence, my appearance had been acknowledged by my father.

Yes, I had inherited his beautiful, sensual, South American mouth! On the whole, I resembled my father more than my mother, as you can tell from the photographs my foster family would later take of me bumping along in the pull cart wearing my white dress, my blue eyes turned brown; and from another one in which I'm sitting on my mother's lap and smiling up at her very sweetly while she gazes down at me with great tenderness.

A full week later, the doctor confirmed I was no longer in mortal danger, but added in the same breath as if attempting to blur the dismal meaning of his next words somewhat: I would need a lot of care.

There lay the sting, the snag, and so the long-awaited words, when the doctor finally uttered them, also brought home a bitter reality: I would need care for the rest of my life, however long or short that would be, but daily, minute by minute, second by second, running parallel to and eating into that one life he himself had been given, for he couldn't multiply the minutes, and every moment of his own life that he dedicated to my care would be lost to literature and posterity.

FOURTEEN

AN UNWRITTEN LAW DICTATES that first time visitors to a baby are to show enthusiasm in front of the parents. Though it is a universal norm, it is applied even more diligently in South American countries than elsewhere, as flattery and compliments are second nature to Latin people. In the tough world of large landowners and their vassals, you fawned or you failed, and flattery was an art passed on from one generation to the next.

The hypocrisy started in Spain, at my birth. We lived in the Madrid neighborhood Argüelles, in the House of Flowers – *Casa de las Flores* – called that way because of the many geraniums hanging from boxes and pots lining the windows, walls and balustrades on all sides. The usual group of friends, poets and diplomats that my father dragged along in his wake from one bar to the next every evening had all turned up. They crowded around my cradle, jostling for position to behold this miracle. The *tertulia* had simply relocated from the bar to my cradle, from the round table to my crib.

I was covered only by a thin sheet, as it was hot in Madrid in August 1934. Only my head peeked out, the top of it hidden by a cap. This had the advantage of optically reducing the size of my head.

But the friends were too smart to be fooled. The cap slipped a little, and before mommy and daddy realized what was happening or could make a move to prevent it, those bending over me had drawn back sharply, bumping up against the outer circle of friends standing around my cradle. The gaps created by the recoiling visitors were quickly filled by the waiting ones moving forward, after which the scene repeated itself, and again, several times. It looked like the swirling water of a stream with a rock in the middle forcing the rushing current to churn its way around it. No one said it, no one dared, but it was obvious that the rock was me; that I was the stumbling-stone.

The compliments and admiring words that my father's friends finally brought out with difficulty were not wasted on him. He glowed with pride, strutting like a peacock. They expressed their approval of me as if they were lifting their glasses for a toast at the bar, words of hope and good wishes slipping glibly from their lips. Mom did not fail to see through their insincerity. Spanish not being her native language, she listened all the more attentively, but the foreign sounds could not mask their revulsion. She also watched their faces, still strange to her. My father was so familiar with their polished and pomaded heads that their disappointment ran off him like water off their oily hair, and he repeated, "She's beautiful, don't you think, isn't she beautiful?"

One of the visitors pushed his way back out of the crowd, away from my cradle, almost knocking over other guests, and loosening his tie, hurried through the living room and the hall to the front door. He ran down the stairs as fast as he could, gasping for breath, and rushed outside. Oh, just another sparkling summer afternoon in Madrid, white doves winging past the balconies and in the corner of your eye a plump female figure on the other side of the road, hair in a bun; trembling leaves on the trees lining the street, sunlight filtering through them glinting in the windows; laundry drying on washing lines, traffic on the distant road; and not a speck of dust or insect in the air, the only fly in the ointment there: over there in the cradle lay a head that seemed ready to burst at the seams, that had chipped the edge of an unsuspecting world, folded the cosmos at a corner. There, everything had been in its proper place that morning: the teacups in the cupboard, the shaving soap beside the tap, the overturned hairbrush next to it. Things were always perfect until they broke, and even if something went missing it didn't really matter. But now a living, breathing head, the head of a child, a newborn baby, lay there throbbing as in a fever, like a swollen wound, bloated with pus and secretion beneath the tulle on his friend's balcony. Were the others putting on an act or was he going mad, was he the only one who saw there was something wrong?

He hastened down the narrow, crowded streets back to his own house at number 3 Velintonia Street, where he wiped the sweat from his forehead, sat at his desk and wrote down what he had seen. Making a solemn vow to himself to never, ever, as long as I lived, as long as my father, my mother, or even he himself lived, publish it:

"We climbed the stairs. 'Come in, Vicente.' A living room. Pablo disappeared. On the far side was a balcony, and behind it a wide slice of sky. I went to the long, narrow terrace, where Pablo was bent over something that looked like a cradle. I watched him from a distance, hearing his voice,

'Malva Marina, can you hear me? Come, Vicente, come! Take a look at this miracle. A girl. The most beautiful girl in the world.'

The words were spouting out of him as I approached. He motioned me to come closer, gazing happily into the cradle. All blissful smiles, blind sweetness of his deep voice, lost in being, in sheer being. I arrived. He straightened up to face me, beaming.

'Look! Look!'

At that moment, the cradle's tulle-trimmed interior revealed its contents: a gigantic head. A relentless head, capable of devouring its own features, it was just that: a cruel head, swollen without mercy, without respite, to the point of losing its purpose. A creature (was it that?) you couldn't look at without pain. A disorderly mass of tissue.

Pale, I lifted my eyes, mumbling some words to him who was expecting them while a false smile covered my face like a mask. Pablo was all light and dreams. He radiated unreality, his delusion as solid as stone, his joyful pride full of gratitude for this heavenly gift," wrote Vicente Aleixandre, a poet and friend of my father's.

;

"A girl. The most beautiful girl in the world." Now I can see myself in the blue onesie, cradled in my father's arm and lifted up to his face, now I look back at his cuddling and cooing, his whispering lips close to my ear. Can you guess which one of us drooled the most? I am lying stretched out on his lap, as if all was as it should be. I dwell on this image often and at length, it makes all else bearable, even if I keep returning to it exactly because it depicts what I lacked. I feel both at the same time: the presence of this reality and its absence. I can sense both the consolation and the sadness of this first embrace.

But where Vicente's description of my appearance is concerned, I can say only this: never trust the notions of poets and their poetic licence, their gross exaggerations! It's just a pity he felt entitled to make such comments about me. Perhaps that is why he decided not to publish them; he knew perfectly well they missed the mark by a mile.

He sat in his room and wrote until the small hours, balcony doors open beside the bed he would soon share with his beloved again. That night, he held her naked body in his arms, feeling immeasurably moved as the side of his hand touched her face, following her perfect shapes, eyes closed, letting his hands find their familiar way over the curves of her body, perfect curves, and lying there with her, flooded with gratitude, thinking himself in prayer as he planted kisses on her, this girl, her long, straight hairs on the sheets, his fingers' pale tips emerging from the tangle. He buried his face between her breasts, put his ear against her chest, listened to the beating of her heart. He lay like this for ages, eyes wide open. The moon had long since risen, its light falling through the net curtain and on the bed, the balcony doors still open. The noises of the nocturnal street came in from outside. Lying there for a long time, he listened to her heartbeat and all the other sounds, and when she turned away from him in her sleep he kept staring motionlessly into the dark, still thinking of what he had seen in the cradle on my father's balcony that afternoon.

You can tell how pompous he could be from his poems, too. Take "Unity in Her":

[...]

Your outward form, diamond or hardened ruby,
brilliance of a blinding sun between my hands,
crater calling me with its inner music,
with your teeth's impenetrable summons.

[...]

Let me gaze and gaze, tinged with love,

[...]

I want to be you, your blood, the roaring lava
bathing your beautiful extremities
while sensing in its confinement life's glorious limits.

This kiss on your lips like a slow thorn,
like a flown-away sea made into a mirror,
like a wing's luster,

[...]

light or death-dealing sword poised threatening above my neck,
but never able to destroy this world's unity.

What were "life's glorious limits"; and what constituted "this world's unity," according to Vicente the poet? Was I part of it, or did I actually detract from it? I still don't know the answers to those questions, which is why I like to consult Szymborska now and again.

Vicente also wrote the poem "Come Always, Come":

Do not come near. Your forehead, your burning forehead, your
    glowing forehead,
traces of kisses,

[...]

I do not want you living within me as light lives,
in the isolation of a star fusing with its light,
being denied love across hard blue space
that separates without uniting,

[...]
Come, come, my love; come, impenetrable forehead, nearly
    rolling roundness

shining like an orbit fated to die in my arms;
come like two eyes or two bottomless solitudes,
two urgent calls from an unknown depth.

Come, come, death, love; come quickly, I will destroy you;
come, I want to kill or love or die or give you everything;
come, rolling like a fickle stone,
like a bewildered moon seeking my rays!

Hey Oskar, Daniel, Lucia, did you hear that? Everyone suffers down there, even the so-called normal people, the flawless, the healthy, the alive-and-kicking! What do you say to that? Was I wrong to see myself as being completely deprived of love, biased to think of everyone else continuously and exclusively bathed in it? Everyone is lonely in love, even in love! Who'd have thought! Just look at them, down there, look at their poems. They teach you that you cannot love and dissolve in love; your loving is done by an "I" that loves, and which is separate from the rest, even your lover; where there is a perfect union, there is no more "I" to experience it.

Lucia replies that I'm trying to console myself with these reflections, but that she's not sure they are much of a consolation. Daniel adds that Aleixandre described his beloved as an "impenetrable forehead"; as "nearly rolling roundness." That couldn't be me, that was my opposite, probably evoked in him by the sight of me that afternoon. I was the Incarnation of human vulnerability; perhaps I reminded him of its existence, which frightened him, perhaps my monstrous outlines were pushing "life's glorious limits"; perhaps I even managed to break up "this world's unity" with my "disorderly mass of tissue," degenerate that I was.

Oskar nods furiously. He also believes I inspired those lines, which Vicente Aleixandre wrote shortly after his visit to our house of flowers and included in his books of poetry, *Pasión de la tierra* and *La destrucción o el amor*, both published in 1935; a year after my birth and a year before the outbreak of the Spanish Civil War.

;

In line with good Latino machismo, my father was highly sensitive to his friends' opinions, and eager to impress them with a presentable wife and children. Perhaps this helped awaken a dormant but steadily growing awareness in him, and perhaps Vicente touched a nerve on that afternoon of his visit, whispering a harsh truth with a glance rather than words ("let me gaze and gaze, tinged with love"); a truth my father would later repeat in his letters, for roughly four weeks later – a month and a day after my birth, to be precise – he wrote about me to a lady friend in very different words; more honest than those to my grandfather. In the space of that first month, when he realized I would always need care and how much trouble it would be to give it, his opinion of me had changed.

"The girl will die, the doctors say; the little thing suffers terribly from the brain hemorrhage she was born with."

"Brain hemorrhage" had a more distinguished ring to it than "hydrocephalus." Blood in the brain sounded so much graver than steadily increasing brain fluid; the former made me a serious, respectable patient, the latter a freak. In the first case, I was the victim of an accident; in the second, I myself would have been the accident.

Another thing strikes me now: perhaps there is not that much difference between the way Vicente looked at his beloved in his poems and that in which my father initially viewed me, when I was still his darling, "the most beautiful girl in the world." Perhaps we were divided by the hard blue space, "that separates without uniting." Perhaps, because I no longer lived in him but had been placed outside of him, like an isolated star, my father wanted to kill or love me too, die or give me everything. Since he could not give me everything – because the world could not give it to me; because I was doomed to always being, always getting, too little – he chose killing, chose dying, as in: not being there for me.

It is in this romantic sense of all-or-nothing – nothing, in my case – that my father's absence seems least incomprehensible to me.

"But don't worry, my dear blonde," my father wrote. "Everything is going fine. The little one has started suckling and the doctors don't visit as often, and she laughs and gains a few grams each day and is making great, martial strides."

My father loved the word "martial," as in "warlike," and the more politically engaged his poems became once he was rid of me, the more it started cropping up in his poetry.

And sometimes Oskar, maybe in an attempt to draw me out rather than make fun of my father, beats martial marches on his afterlife tin drum; marches that I nip in the bud by plonking the full weight of my body on top of his drum.

Oh Hagar, you'll find out when your time comes: the hereafter is all about going over old ground.

FIFTEEN

SOCRATES, TROTTING NEXT TO ME on a ram, suddenly fixes me with a serious eye. A frown that has taken over his whole face has driven his lecherous satyr's look into the shady thicket. He opens his mouth to speak, and for a moment I think I can even see a goatee beard trembling at his chin, but I soon realize it's just the shadow of his jaw.

"Malva," he begins, "on accepting my death sentence, I asked myself, and my judges, just what was so bad about death; for surely, it would either be a long sleep or another life in a different place, where, unlike on earth, I would be allowed to practice philosophy and search for what is good and true. Luckily, the latter turned out to be the case, and as I had hoped, I've been able to surround myself with the noblest of heart and purest of mind. I've also encountered your father here, and of course couldn't help subjecting him to my investigations into whether he considers himself a wise man when he is not. In life he habitually took the moral high ground in matters he considered just or unjust, so I asked him to his face, 'Dear Neruda, if you really believe that all people are equal and that you are duty-bound to speak for the weak and the voiceless, how come you banished and concealed your own daughter, who was, after all, weak and in need of help? Is it not a father's duty to care for his child, even if that child does not live up to the standards and expectations of the majority?'"

Socrates is so generous as to tell me my father's answer to this.

Neruda: "Dear Socrates, of course it was my duty, just as it was yours to look after your children. You had three of them, three sons, the youngest two of which were only small children when you left your earthly life behind and entered the realm of the dead. Nevertheless, you chose hemlock over caring for them, even though your friends offered you many ways of escaping your sentence. Had you fled, they would have protected you, paid for your crossing, found a place for you to stay. You and your wife and children could have moved away quietly, to stay with a friend of Kriton's, or one of the many others who would gladly have taken you under their wing. Since you didn't choose to take that path, who are you to tell me now that I should have handled things differently with Malva?"

Socrates: "Did I, by any chance, cast out one of my children and then continue to lead a happy life without giving that child another thought? By no means! I chose death because all other alternatives would have made life as a philosopher impossible to me anyway, and my children would have suffered from that, too. As it was, they at least had the memory of a father who died honorably. But in all modesty, it's not me I want to talk about but you, given that you always claimed to strive for justice – so does an anonymous passerby have a right to a good and fair life simply because they are a passerby, and does it matter whether they are an anonymous passerby or your daughter, since everyone has an equal right to a good and fair life?"

Neruda: "Alas, Socrates, in my daughter's case, a good life was never in the cards; she was incurably ill."

Socrates: "But does the anonymous passerby with an incurable illness not have the same right to a good and fair life as the anonymous passerby without an incurable illness?"

Neruda: "They both have an equal right to a good and fair life."

Socrates: "If everyone has the same right to a good life and just treatment, does it not follow that your daughter has the same right to a good life and just treatment as the anonymous passerby?"

Neruda: "My daughter has as much right to be treated fairly as anyone else."

Socrates: "So how come you, who considered yourself wise and just when you were on earth, did not look after your daughter?"

Neruda: "I believe, like you do, that a man must strive for justice as far as possible, but I have never given any guarantees as to the outcome of my striving. Writing my poetry, I was merely stating an intention."

Socrates: "But you did declare yourself the spokesman of the oppressed, and you passed judgement on others."

Neruda: "The oppressed have a right to a spokesman as well, even one who doesn't live up to his own standards. A lawyer does not need to be completely blameless himself, as long as he does the best possible job of defending the person he represents."

Socrates: "Would your daughter not have benefited more from such representation? Or perhaps this representation would have had the disadvantage of taking place in anonymity, without an audience, while you sought applause and approval? Perhaps looking after your daughter would have earned you too little praise, while standing up for the anonymous masses generated all the more recognition for being part of a movement, a political direction that was very popular in your days?"

Neruda: "The great task I set myself, just as you did with your philosophy, certainly played a part. Poetry was my mission and vocation. Besides, I was able to help more people with my poetry than I would have been if I had dedicated myself exclusively to my daughter's care."

Socrates: "But if that honor you took such pains to achieve is partly being canceled out now, what good has it done?"

Neruda: "At least there was some honor involved. If I had spent all my time looking after my daughter, there would have been none;

I would not even have had the honor of this conversation with you now, as you would not have deemed me interesting enough for your Socratic Dialogue."

Socrates: "Dear Neruda, to me, all conversation partners are of equal interest, I do not dismiss anyone in advance, I give everyone a fair chance to prove to me that they've got hold of the right end of the stick and I the wrong one, but sadly I am yet to meet the person who can convince me I am wrong, and you, Neruda, have not succeeded either. It pains me that I will have to tell this to your daughter, since you refuse to meet her face to face."

Neruda: "My most highly esteemed Socrates, at court, when you refused the offered escape routes and chose hemlock over exile, you did not face your children either; you claimed you did not want them present so as to avoid a display of maudlin self-pity that you considered beneath a man with an elevated reputation such as yours. The same thing goes for me. I want to spare everyone the embarrassing, shameful spectacle of a reunion with my daughter, the mawkish scene of our embrace, and so on. It would be kitsch of the highest order, especially if it were enforced. I would never be capable of carrying out such an embrace sincerely with cameras pointed at me from all sides and you breathing your philosophical comments down my neck. I'd rather enter eternity alone and wander around it aimlessly forever; I prefer exile to such an indignity. I bid you goodbye, dear Socrates – you lead your death the way you think fit, and please let me do the same."

SIXTEEN

SHORTLY AFTER MY BIRTH in Madrid, a certain female head started popping up more and more frequently among the others, a blonde one with a pale face. I can still see her bending over my cradle. My father had repeated his María Luisa Bombal trick, convincing my mother it would be good if someone came to live with us, someone to look after her in her fragile state.

I can still hear the woman with the carillon name, whose unceasing Siren bray about politics, campaigns, Communism and political activism against the great global injustices disturbed the peace of my early youth, noisily pursuing my father, leaving him nowhere to go except toward her as she penetrated into the farthest corners of sentences that said one thing and meant another, piercing the moments of silence between my parents; and the moments when I cried. Those, especially.

He had met her at one of the many meetings he went to when we lived in Madrid, shortly after my birth. He spotted her in his favorite bar, went up to her, sat down beside her, put an arm around her shoulder, and they sat that way for a long time, without saying or doing anything.

Ah yes, doña Delia: if anyone has grace and beauty, she does. The eyes of women turn away jealously. The eyes of men follow her full of lust. She is a magnet, and everywhere she goes, every room she enters, whether she lets her voice ring out like the peal of carillon bells or keeps silently in the background, she draws everyone's attention to herself; especially my father's, even if he is seated at some long table or standing in a corner half concealed behind his dull and oh so ordinary wife who, almost hidden by her hat and not half as desirable as she used to be, recently became a mother.

Every afternoon from the moment of their first meeting sometime during that glaring Indian summer of 1934, their favorite bar Cervezería de Correos became the port of call and mooring site for their amorous rendezvous, and it was there they laid the gangway to embark on the ship of night, whispering and murmuring plans about what the rest of the evening and night might bring. Visits to the theater or the cinema, talks in Carlos Morla Lynch's house; romantic dinners at La Granja Enar on Alcalá Street or fat calamari fried in olive oil on semi-sweet bread rolls from a stall – all of those were regularly chalked up on the freshly enamored couple's slate. Strolling from one place to the next through the shimmering heat of nocturnal Madrid, a bottle of *chinchón* tucked under one arm, they held mysterious conversations about art and lust, love and politics. At every corner they bumped into people they knew, who would trail after the two as if stuck to the Golden Goose, and soon they formed a group rather than a couple, moving through the streets and squares on the next leg of their nocturnal journey. It took some doing, but in the end the two geese usually managed to shake off their following with strategically craned necks, meaningful glances, whisperings and tête-à-tête warblings that shut out anyone outside a radius of just a few centimeters. (With hindsight, my spirit eye could of course penetrate their protective shield with ease, but I really have better things to do than eavesdrop on those two slobbering soaks.) Often enough, their body language was all it took – when their fingers interlaced and they only had eyes and ears for each other, their backs turned to the rest, in some bar or other. After which, arms still linked, legs getting shaky, they proceeded to The Devil, a nightclub at 60 Atocha Street where Mario Carreño manned the bar, a young Cuban with an endless supply of witticisms. The champagne, wines and cider were uncorked. The Lecuona Orchestra played fiery music, composed by musician friends of theirs and conducted by maestro Ríos. Half-naked girls let their hair down to The Dance of Cocaine and Tits of Sand, the Afro-Cuban rhythms staged to sound like hell, and there were dance competitions for the so-called riotous parishioners.

Ding-dong bing-a-bang-bong. Electrifying!

Delia's ancestor don Juan Vásquez del Carril y del Carril, inhabitant of Camariñas, a small bay on the Spanish La Coruña coast, had left Spain in the eighteenth century for what was now Argentina, just as my mother's ancestor, the governor-general Jeremias van Riemsdijk, had sailed from Holland to the Dutch East Indies, today's Indonesia.

King Carlos III of Spain had appointed don Juan Vásquez del Carril y del Carril as royal mayor and alderman of San Juan, territory that belonged to Chile at the time (for all his sympathy with the fate of the penniless, ordinary man, when it came to choosing a wife, my father was initially partial to women with a distinguished family tree).

To give you an idea of how things stood with the Carril family at the time: Delia's grandfather had once taken out an advertisement in the paper in which he publicly washed his hands of his wife's spending habits.

And it's true, she was dressed to the nines! The whole house, too, including the garden and the gallery, was always decked out; especially on holidays, for which all members of the extended family showed up, primped and preened in bows and ties. Her family was both insanely rich and abjectly destitute, the fatal accidents and cases of suicide (such as her father's after the death of his mother, the squanderous spender and generous giver) piling up like tragic acrobats – and in this she also resembled my mother, though by that time the Hagenaars had sunk deeper into poverty than the Carrils.

If only they had known of the similarity of their backgrounds; it might have sparked a little more empathy for my mother in Delia. But Delia's father had presented her with a horse when she was only four years old, and this hugely appreciated fatherly gift had instilled her with a fearlessness that made her different from all the other girls in the whole world.

Her recent conversion to Communism had presented Delia del Carril, a born, raised and lapsed aristocrat, pushing fifty autumns but still blooming with the youthful brilliance of thirty summers which made the twenty year age difference between her and my father almost unnoticeable (honest, it was!), with a purpose in life that she, childless, adventurous, averse to marriage and tired of her empty, idle aristocratic existence, had never found elsewhere.

Oh, but I say this now with the outrage of the outcast, the derision of the disowned and the jealousy of the rejected, for they stood on the right side, my father and Delia, and as an objective, all-knowing observer, I have to admit to the fact they later saved two thousand Spanish political refugees from French concentration camps and shipped them to Chile on board the ship the *Winnipeg*. It was a feat of pure heroism in which the daredevilish Delia was his dauntless muse and helpmate in the struggle against injustice and oppression and yes, I can't deny that, while her voice grates on my ears at other times, the way she lead and prompted him to do such courageous deeds was very laudable. And she accomplished all that in spite of her clumsiness, for she was so absent-minded she tossed matches into the soup while cooking and tried to pay for bus tickets with buttons, which actually quite endears her to me. And again, oh my friend Goethe, two souls dwell in my deceased breast: that of the incensed daughter, abandoned and deprived of fatherly love, and that of the long-suffering omniscient narrator, but, oh Goethe, as Hagar's father also quotes you, "Every consequence leads to the Devil." It is one reason, if not *the* reason, that I have a right to exist with hydrocephalus!

Doña Delia, oh! daring, dashing, death-defying, dauntless daredevil Doña Delia – my father couldn't stop saying your name in the first months after I was born, and when I visited him after my death he still hadn't tired of you, and wouldn't for a full two decades – I ask you now, from the bottom of my silent heart, from the furthest reaches of my knowing soul: why, why, *why* did you travel to Madrid three months before my parents arrived, just three months before I started my pale, pathetic, pitiful existence, to add your pealing voice of a former Argentinian aristocrat to the ranks of the Communists in a city that was practically under siege? And why didn't you quickly spur on that horse of yours and gallop out of our lives forever?

;

A visitor called when my father was out. Our front door was open. He found my mother behind it, sitting alone at my bedside, as she did all day. She told him my father had gone to the cinema with Delia del Carril (ding-dong bing bang-bong-bing: by that time she had all but moved in with us, under the pretext of caring for my mother after the exhausting birth, but actually so as to be near my father).

Meanwhile, in the loneliness of the apartment, my mother would be trying to get me to drink cod-liver oil, which I, who declined all kinds of fluid, naturally refused as well; while my father, sitting in a bar with his friends the Poets of '27 and The Carillon, never refused any drink put in front of him, on the contrary; he drank to Madrid, to poetry, to freedom and to his friends. Their number increased as steadily and unstoppably as the circumference of my head.

"*¡Salud!*"
"To your health! To your health! To your health!"
"To everyone's health!"

For all that is, and all that is visible, is multiplied. But she, seated at that other window, remained in the dark, invisible, unnoticed, and it was exactly as the fellow socialist and poet Berthold Brecht wrote in his *Three Penny Opera*: that some are in the darkness and others in the light, and that we only see those in the light because the others are out of sight. And now, after my death, I see both, and watch carefully, moving from light to dark and from the dark into the light. I report on everything I see. Not a single comma escapes me.

But between the light and the dark there was always the twilight, the *crepúsculo* whose praises my father had sung and that was of the same beauty and blazing colors as the end of the night or break of day, the *madrugada* – the moment when the fanatical drinkers who hadn't been shaken off arrived at Casa de las Flores (while my mother and I were trying to sleep in the next room) to conclude the party with a nightcap, and part ways at the first sound of birdsong.

Twenty eventful years later, my father exchanged Delia for Matilde, la Patoja, and justified it by saying that Matilde was only doing to Delia what she herself had done to Marietje, my mother, and that therefore she had no right to complain. It was the moment when the twilight carousel left the carillon.

SEVENTEEN

"WHY DON'T YOU COME TO MADRID?" Federico asked my father when they were still living in Buenos Aires and my mother was pregnant with me. "That's where it happens!"

When my father-to-be arrived in Madrid by train shortly before my birth, Federico was waiting for him on the platform, a shy smile on his lips and a flower in his hand.

No matter how many times my father would be picked up later by other writers and poets, no matter how many train stations all over the world thronged with crowds to welcome him; in his mind's eye, he would always see the diffident, short, smiling figure of Federico carrying that single flower in his hand; because after Federico had been shot by a death squad, my father still saw him on each of his travels, his escapes, and in exile, a ghostly vision waiting for him at every destination to hand him that flower.

In Madrid, my father recited his poetry for the first time.

"Bring your Javanese masks," Federico the dramaturgist suggested. My father took the masks he and my mother had bought in Java together and placed them on wooden poles beside him. He gave his first recital hiding his face behind one of them. The dark bronze sonorous sounds coming from behind the mask resonated deep, low and heavy in the insides of the audience – they vibrated and swarmed, awe-inspiring, compelling, chilling. Like a howl from the depths of the soul, a plea for help that was irresistible.

No one who has never heard his voice will ever understand how urgent the plea of that voice was, how impossible to resist.

Forget all his poems. Listen to his voice and you will understand all the better why my mother did not refuse his proposal of marriage.

Words; compliant, persuasive, engaging at first; then becoming harsh, negative, contemptuous, but all spoken in that same voice. Why did he not modify it when the meaning of his words changed so dramatically? Why, from his first declarations of love to his ultimate words of rejection and renunciation, did he utter everything in the same decisive, peremptory tone?

My father's first public poetry recital in Madrid had such an impact that it was followed by a constant stream of invitations. The audience squeezed into the last corner of every venue, he spoke to sold-out football stadiums.

When the miners revolted in Spain, it reminded my father of miners' strikes in Chile. His friend Lorca's execution by firing squad made him realize that he wanted to join Communism, to fight against fascism. One day, he recited verses from *España en el corazón* – the poems he wrote during and about the Civil War – in Santiago's central market because he hadn't prepared a speech, and by the end, even the toughest worker was in tears. From that moment on, he considered himself the spokesman of the common man. Bringing his poetry to the simple, everyday people, offering his poems like bread; under the circumstances, this is what he believed was needed.

;

The martial strides rang out ever more clearly. They became the sound of marching soldiers. My father no longer deemed Madrid to be a safe place for my mother and me.

Here, between the reeking nappies, chewed-up rubber nipples and stuffed toys flung out of the pram, that one sense of the word martial died. And there, on the battleground of the Republicans and Falangists, under the fluttering flags, the beating drums and the soldiers' clarion calls, the other martial rose like a sun that set the world ablaze, a red sun rising so proudly, so full of courage. And while the one martial gobbled up the other like Pac-Man, a smiley with fangs, my father was preparing his escape from us.

Early June 1936, he found a convenient excuse in the approaching civil war to pack my mother and me on a train to Barcelona, leaving him unencumbered and free to spend the next twenty years of his life in the company of his sonorous mistress Delia, alias The Carillon. In one of his next letters to her, he, an avid collector of model boats, ordered her to buy a model boat he had seen on the way, "because I am here in the Nautique hotel in Marseille, surrounded by sailing ships. I am certain we are heading for a happy future together. I'm so glad to be rid of Maruca. This morning, I clipped my own nails, tricky though it was."

;

I was almost two years old when, instead of being cured of my hydrocephalus, I was banished from my father's house. It started on the platform with the usual fussing around with luggage, the waving, the goodbyes and all the other empty gestures. A flawlessly mimed show of sorrow, that waving. There was the well-known moment when the train set itself in motion and puff puffed away to become a speck moving out of my father's view; completely dissolving into the horizon. The heat was oppressive. In Barcelona, we visited Barend van Tricht, an acquaintance of my mother's who had been a witness at my parents' wedding in Batavia, and lodged at a boarding house for four months. Finally, my father visited on November 10 of that year to announce his decision that though he would not be able to travel with us, we should leave the country. He didn't tell us how he envisaged the future.

We traveled to Monaco with the Van Trichts before continuing to The Hague in the Netherlands, where my mother found a room in another boarding house (she would only ever live in boarding houses from then on), and where, another two years later, she gave me up to a foster family in Gouda so she could go back to work. And because it was a Christian Science family, she was secretly hoping I would be cured by some divine intervention or other.

Under the influence of his political engagement, my father wrote "Song for the Mothers of Slain Militiamen," the soldiers who had died for the good cause during the Civil War. He himself called it his first "proletarian poem":

mothers pierced by anguish and death,
look at the heart of the noble day that is born,
and know that your dead ones smile from the earth
raising their fists above the wheat.

It was worlds removed from my death in the Netherlands several years later, and from my mother. I did not smile from the earth, I did not raise my fists above the wheat. There was nothing hopeful about my death. I had not died for something greater or better than myself, nor sacrificed my healthy body for my home country. My mother was not the mother of a hero, whose heroism reflected on her even after the death of her child, whose valor brought her solace, admiration, respect – and my father's odes. No, I had not been a testament to an education in virtue, I had only been myself. I had been less than myself, I had been sickly. There was little poetic honor to be gained from accounts of my life, my illness and my death. There was little honor to be gained from me. No Amen.

From now on, our history becomes the story of detachment, a blind arm of a river that branches off from the great stream of life only to run dry. No matter how heroically I fought for my life, I wouldn't make it in the end.

My father knew that, and he couldn't bear it. He could only bear death if it was the result of a courageous struggle, not if it occurred in spite of the struggle, not if defeat was inevitable from the outset and could not be averted.

The war in Spain went from bad to worse, but the spirit of resistance among the Spanish people had spread all over the world. "In the history of the intellect there has not been a subject as fertile for poets as the Spanish war. The blood spilled in Spain was a magnet that sent shudders through the poetry of a great period," my father wrote in his memoirs. The spirit of resistance touched him, too. He sent us away. He had long since found a new ideal to live for. Ding-dong bing-bang.

Ever since the first time I heard my father beg for his next model boat, which he did in the same letter as he told his new love of his relief to get away from us, I have often scurried over to Roald Dahl's writing hut. He has an afterlife duplicate of it. Outside is a swimming pool with no water. Dahl is wading through the withered leaves on the bottom, making swimming motions in the air with his arms. When he spots me, he climbs out of the empty swimming pool and beckons me to come closer. He offers me biscuits and pours lemonade, then sits down on the chair opposite to tell me the whole story all over again. I listen with bated breath. I don't let him skip a single detail.

Some of the things he keeps in his hut remind me of my

father's collections; model toys, shells; but among the shells on the windowsill, there's also a piece of bone from his own hip. Old Mr. Dahl points, and once again I follow his finger to the mysterious object I particularly admire: a small, fragile tube, no wider than a pipette. It is a yellowed specimen of the Wade-Dahl-Till shunt; a small tube with a valve with which excessive brain fluid can be drained from the heads of young hydrocephalus patients. Dahl designed it himself when he was alive, with the help of a toy maker and a doctor. He tells me about it again and again, dishing up the gory details like a grateful storyteller who, after being deprived of an audience for a long time, has finally found a child to talk to. He waved me over the first time he saw me: on earth, his son Theo had developed exactly such a hydrocephalus after being hit by a car, at a time when there was insufficient medical treatment available for children. The existing shunts kept getting blocked. By contrast, the miniature engines designed by hydraulic engineer and toy maker Stanley Wade, who also built model trains and aeroplanes, never blocked or jammed, and this gave Dahl the idea to ask the model train maker and old acquaintance of his to help him develop a medical innovation. The result was published in *The Lancet*, and was actually used on a couple of thousand children until a better shunt was introduced. I hang on his every word to the end.

The tube reminds me of the pipe in which the glutton Augustus Gloop gets stuck in *Charlie and the Chocolate Factory*, another story Dahl tells me.

"Exactly," he exclaims delightedly when I tell him of my association.

"I always draw my inspiration from reality. Pity your father, for all his passion for model boats, didn't think of that."

EIGHTEEN

ON SUMMER DAYS, I would rumble along in my pull cart to the Reeuwijk Lakes just outside Gouda with my foster family. My foster father Julsing pulled me all the way on the long, bumpy, winding road, his forehead beaded with sweat, while Heika, Geesje and little Fred, my foster sisters and brother, ran around the cart like mad, horsing about and whining in vain for their turn to pull it.

Legs stretched, I let myself be chauffeured around all the livelong day like a princess. If I'd actually been one, I bet that giant heads would have become the rage, just as the abnormally small feet of one Imperial concubine led to centuries of girls' feet being crippled by foot-binding in China. Celebrities often set an example. Who knows what inventive methods of head enlargement would have become fashionable? (Dahl and I have thought of many.) Luckily, I came from a humble background, and no one suspected my father would become one of the greatest poets of the century.

We arrived at the water's edge, and I was carefully lowered into it. Foster father Julsing lifted me out of my pull cart, and I could see the muscles of his strong arms flex as he bent down until my stiff legs were completely submerged by a blanket of soft green water. At that point I'd start to crow. As happy as the idiot in the bath, who "has not lost the wisdom of the body / and does not need the wisdom of the mind." I would gladly have sat in the water forever, only my head bobbing on the surface.

I stayed in Gouda for the rest of my childhood until, aged eight, I drew my last breath like an enormous air bubble blown up to bursting point in imitation of my head.

As you can imagine, my dark hair and olive-colored skin made me stand out among the children of my Gouda foster family, all of whom had downy, pale-peach cheeks and wheat-blonde hair. My distinctive appearance emphasized my special status, quite apart from my other physical traits and defects which, while they hindered me, didn't actually frustrate me very much as I was hardly aware of my own limitations. I did suffer from a recurring pain in my head that felt like a sword splitting my skull from top to bottom and which always came on unexpectedly. I couldn't talk, I couldn't use my arms, I couldn't stand or walk. Sitting upright took a huge effort, as there was always that heavy head to carry on my slender neck like Atlas bearing the heavens on his shoulders. Put bluntly: I was named after a plant and I vegetated.

However, I'm proud to say that I had a good singing voice. A small, golden-voiced reptile, that was me. Long before other children would have been able to talk, I sang along with my mother. My dear mother, who took the train from The Hague to Gouda every month to babble at me for an hour, to sing to me and hug me; my beautiful mother, who my foster sisters called "a really good-looking lady." I always looked forward to seeing her sweet face, her beautifully made-up mouth painted with red lipstick, and her shiny black hair. In her presence, adrift on her lap, I forgot how much my head weighed me down.

The children held their breath until the moment they heard my happy crowing. It was the signal that they could let out their own shrieks and send them skimming across the surface of the shallow lake as they paddled and splashed each other with water. Afterwards, they would hang their soaking clothes out to dry on the railing of my pull cart. On the way home we formed a caravan, like a ship in the desert, and everyone joined in the singing. Even I sang along. It is one of my most cherished memories of my childhood on earth.

;

I was lucky, by the way, to be housed in Gouda. Had I ended up a few hundred kilometers to the east, in a neighboring country that was more than a little menacing at the time, the bell would have tolled much sooner for that head of mine, so loud it would even have drowned out the sound of its sloshing water. We hydrocephalics were second on their stamp-out-the-disabled wish list. In the Nazis' view, only the mongols were more deserving of death. Life to them was as pure as a huge, snow white sheet. Not everyone was welcome to sleep under it – not people like me, for instance, who would only paw at it with their grimy fingers and leave stains that even the soapsuds of truth wouldn't be able to remove.

I admit that I, too, would of course have preferred having Marlene Dietrich's looks and perfectly symmetrical face, but wanting to do away with me just because of my inordinate disproportionality really is beyond the pale; and then to think that an eminent academic had written a scholarly piece about great German poets, composers and thinkers who almost qualified as being hydrocephalic, such as Beethoven and Schopenhauer. In that article, the author argues that there is a thin line between genius and degeneration, that the two have even been known to overlap; one significant example being Nietzsche in his last years, in turn infused by Wagner's genius (yet another ugly man with a huge head).

Incidentally, the parents of the handicapped children knew nothing of the snuffing out that was going on there, in a darkness they hadn't yet glimpsed; they thought they had entrusted their children safely to the care of nursing homes, not delivered them into the hands of child murderers. It was a misunderstanding that the friendly nursing staff deliberately perpetuated in the reassuring letters they wrote to the parents: "Onno is improving by the day, he can already scamper along holding my hand," "Eva eats small pieces of apple now," even if the little patients had long since been murdered, to which their own carers had given the order by including "—" in their nursing report; the secret code of that damned golden section, this time translated into runes. And though I often complain about my name and the fact my father never mentioned it once in his two-inch thick memoirs, at least I *had* one – prisoners in German concentration camps were given only a number.

But of course you already know that. When your cousin Marja was small, your uncle Nonie would take her on his lap time and time again to show her his arm and ask, "Who did this?" And every time, she gave the same, correct answer: "The Krauts did that."

;

It is a blessing in disguise that I was unaware of my disproportionality during my short, mist-shrouded life on earth, because otherwise Gouda itself would have acted as a constant reminder. It was the city of Gouda smoking pipes, Gouda cheese, Gouda stained glass, Gouda waffles, Gouda candles and the Gouda Weigh House; different materials with specific shapes and dimensions that the local population was keen to identify with. The famous Gouda cheeses are shaped in molds, which are called *kaaskoppen*, cheese heads; a name, incidentally, that refers to their shape and not the color, summer blonde, which cheese has in common with many Dutch people. If only there had been a mold for my head when I was being made; then I would have met all requirements.

Looking back, I see them everywhere, the shapes, measurements, and weights that seem to be the cornerstones the city was built on. That was of course down to the trade conducted in Gouda to which the city owed its fame and fortune. Where there is trade, there are plenty of measures, standards, conditions and agreements, and to prevent fraud, every weight is painstakingly calibrated.

My pull cart trundled past market stalls and shop windows where material value was made manifest in the most marvelous displays of goods, objects and tools. Bumpity-bump I went, over the cobblestones. I looked around, eyes popping out of my head – literally, as the pressure on my brains squeezed them out a little, making one eye bulge slightly to the side. I looked a bit like one of those small, overbred dogs you see everywhere these days: Chihuahuas. I couldn't see very well, or make much sense of what I did see.

But nowadays, I don't miss a thing. Now, I can see the black haze shrouding the city, paradoxically enough caused by the pursuit of purity and perfection; a by-product of chasing after an ideal of edelweiss whiteness, pitch black bits of charred paper blew through the streets all the way from bombed-out Rotterdam. Everything that had once glittered yellow and gold, Gouda's glory, had now turned old, grey, dark and withered. The Market Square was empty; the golden-yellow cheeses all gone.

Boldly blowing away the haze lying over the city, I can see the things in their handmade, flawed excellence again, and I can also see myself in all my endearing unwieldiness (pull cart) trundling past them (my head casting a shadow on the street like Quasimodo's hunch).

In the shop windows, I spy some Gouda waffles, easily recognizable by their perfectly round shape. All the candy that sweetened my youth was as circular as the face of a clock: waffles, lollipops, King brand peppermints, rolls of licorice and the equally round

Napoleon balls.

Rolling along my memories of my time on earth now, which I am only just starting to understand, I read on the facade of The Salmon restaurant on Gouda Market Square: "Not too high, not too low, but exactly right." The owner had the sarcastic text chiseled into a plaque in the front wall after the city council thwarted his plans to build The Salmon taller than the neighboring Weigh House. The council wouldn't allow anything to tower above the Weigh House, the true church of the merchant city. Had I been able to read, I would also have read this:

A weight too heavy or too light
Is abhorrent in His sight;
A falseness in the weighing bowl
Corrupts man's honor, and his soul.

It was the inscription to the high relief which once adorned the front of the old Weigh House of Gouda and showed the weighing of the cheeses.

Pondering over these words now, I realize what my designated place was in life: in the eyes of the others, I was a fault in the goods. I was "too heavy, too light." I had cheated by existing anyway. I had hoodwinked my parents. I had been tampered with. I was born damaged, but came at the same price – my birth – as any other baby. Where were the gatekeepers, the cheese weighers and executioners who had allowed this to happen?

;

In front of the church, a couple of old men took a few final puffs at their Gouda pipes, skilfully carved in the form of miniature heads –

roly-poly, plump-cheeked little faces – and trapping the smoke for a moment before blowing it out in a stream, the pipe smokers' cheeks were just as puffed-out as those of the decorative carvings.

Having performed their round-cheeked pipe-head imitations to each other, the men, still snorting with laughter, entered the church to look at the famous Gouda windows; patting each other on the back as they pointed out the stained-glass scenes with their walking sticks. I, too, now saw the freedom of conscience, the births of John the Baptist and Jesus, the twelve-year-old Jesus in the temple, Jonah and the whale, Balaam and the talking donkey, the Apostles, the arrest, the mocking, Jesus presented to the people by Pilate, the carrying of the cross, the resurrection, the ascension and the descent of the Holy Ghost. The actual meaning of those windows had always eluded me, but I enjoyed basking in the square of colorful light they threw on the walls – the shadows of shadows, and my head dancing among them. Eyes half closed, I could see the colors blend into each other. All my foster parents had to do was park my pull cart somewhere close to such a square of light, and I was no trouble at all.

They are still there, the stained-glass windows in the church of Gouda; located high above the people gathered below, forcing them to lift their eyes up to heaven to catch a glimpse of their beauty. At such a distance, it's impossible to see what exactly they depict.

"You lowly mortals don't deserve any better than standing down below," the windows say. From where I am now, I can hear them very clearly.

"Otherwise, you'd only get ideas above your station! Don't forget that even you, the spared ones, the blessed, those endowed with brains not weighed down by excessive fluid, the quiz winners and lottery millionaires, must look up to us with humbleness and deference, fully aware of your relative unimportance and mortality," the high-pitched, thin-voiced chorus sneers.

Shoo! Shut up, hold your big traps – you don't know any more than we do!

At first, I was angry with my father for not writing a single word about me (lower lip in a pout, sulky frown, petulantly kicking the limp lines of his poetry), but not only have I come to terms with my non-appearance, today I can even see its advantages. By not describing me in any way, he has not pinned me down, either. I am given the last word about myself, and, in regard to his writing, the ultimate and definitive one.

A rewriting of the natural and religious order according to Malva: just as in the beginning there was the word, there will be the word at the end. If the first is by the creator, whom nothing can surpass in greatness, the second is the creation, small and infirm, passing her final verdict (Malva's beautiful Last Judgement).

Of course, you must take my claim that I believe in a last word – an Ultimate Word; mine – with a pinch of salt. I would like to, but I'm too unsteady, I never learned to walk. I'm trying out my thoughts and my voice as I speak and write. After all, I don't believe in perfection.

I've already told you about Goethe. On earth, he was given the use of a garden in Sicily by an Italian patron, and as he examined the plants, looking for common traits, he noticed that each one of them consisted of an archetypal form repeated in its parts. Some believe that Goethe's discovery ties in with the "golden section" theory. According to this doctrine, a divine ratio can be found in art, nature and science; one true ratio that is thought to govern everything in nature and the universe, from the proportions of the human body to those of leaves and flowers, from the curves of seashells to the orbits that planets trace through outer space. Renaissance artists used it to reproduce the proportions of the human body and to draw buildings in perspective. A hidden code was thought to give access to this secret.

Which is exactly what Goethe did not mean! The belief in the existence of perfection is the source of almost all evil, I can tell you, for its downside is the belief in a scapegoat. It lies at the root of our pursuit of that perfection, of eugenics, social Darwinism, national-socialist desire for purity, fascism, religious fanaticism and much more of all the evil in which humans surpass animals – everything they have knowingly inflicted, and still inflict, on each other. This is, insofar as I am capable of firmness, my firm conviction. Even though the philosopher Socrates claimed that no one does evil knowingly. If Socrates were right, humans would be on the same moral level as plants and animals, who really are incapable of knowingly doing evil. To my mind, humans differ from all other life forms on earth exactly because they do have that choice; the golden section determines who or what belongs or does not belong, and those who do not belong are ignored at best and destroyed at worst, as justified by some ludicrous theory or other.

Beauty and truth are apparently only a matter of the correct proportions. No one knows more about that than I do. And in the end, the golden-ratio-snobs are probably right – after all, I didn't die prematurely from my hydrocephalus for nothing.

;

"Malva?" I heard someone say.

"Shhh. She's asleep, she sleeps sitting up, head tipped to one side a little, leaning on the railing of her pull cart. Can you see her eyeballs rolling from side to side behind her eyelids? It means she's dreaming."

"What about, do you think?"

"The mud? Being hungry?"

"Look, there's the faint smile that always plays around her lips; isn't it funny, how she always seems to be smiling about a joke we don't know, that no one knows. What do you think *she* knows?"

"I've no idea – do you?"

"Malvalalala."

"Shush now, you'll wake her up."

"She's such an mystery, with her funny looks; she keeps everything inside, but I can tell she's always watching. She just can't speak, that's all."

"But she's such a sweet girl. So downy. I was a little afraid of her at first, but she's a sweet little monster."

"She's our mascot."

"Yes, cos mom and dad took her home from church."

"This church?"

"No, the other one, where they always sing psalms too – the big church of Mary Baker Eddy in The Hague. When we go there, Nel looks after her."

"Nel Nel Caramel."

"Shush!"

We played at "making Malva better," which was, after all, the desired effect of my stay with the Christian Science family. Prayers and songs were performed around my cot. I may not be able to think for myself, my foster mother reasoned, but if others prayed and sang for me, it might just sway God's mercy.

And sure enough, I made progress, as my mother reported in her letters to my father. They were upbeat and optimistic, while carefully omitting any mention of the religious beliefs of the family that had so nobly taken me into their – already crowded – midst; my father loathed religion.

Opium for the people.

But then not everyone can afford the luxury of disbelief. I was ill, there was a war, my mother suffered poverty and my father hardly sent her any money. Under the circumstances, she opted for the opium and hoped for a miracle. No one was to know at the time that her misery would later drive her to actual opium and morphine.

Look, mommy: the miracle has happened after all! Admittedly only after my death, but let's not split hairs; a miracle is a miracle.

;

Despite the war, everything in the Julsing household took its usual steadfast course, like a pull cart on a lonely country lane. There was a painting by Ferdinand Bol at the Museum of Gouda called "Man with High Cap." My mother, quite possibly inspired by it, knitted a cap for me that did a reasonably good job of covering the excessive bulge that was my head, so that I wouldn't be teased by other children in the street and gaped at whenever I was taken outdoors.

Thinking back to this, seeing my mother knitting the white cap on her lap, moves me deeply. It is details like this, the unnecessary, unneeded, pointless, vain labors of love, that betray true affection, and I am as touched by it as the historian who, reading Dante, was struck by the tiny word "Bice" – the nickname of Dante's mistress – hidden away in one of his poems, from which he concluded that Beatrice must actually have existed. If only my father had done the same for me, hidden my name in some of his poems, or at least a diminutive of it. As it is, he only mentions me once, in a poem – but since mine's just one in an endless list of names, it doesn't count. Such details, let me tell you, are what it is all about, not the immaculate proportions of the golden section or a big gesture or genetic purity or eternal truth or the Nobel Prize for Literature. But what do I know? I'm long dead, after all.

At this point I'm interrupted by Lucia, who is my bosom friend in the afterlife and as vain as a film star. She just has to let us know, again, that her own name is a reference to Dante's Lucia, and that in her father's eyes, this is who she always remained.

She whispered it in the ear of her earthly biographer: her father loved her dearly from the moment she was born – to him, she was not mad. He disagreed with everyone who said otherwise. No matter what others thought about her, James never lost sight of his daughter's beauty and talent. He could see the desperation of her life but refused to leave her in the lurch. In his view, she never lost the qualities he spotted in her at birth, when he compared her to Dante's Beatrice: "Once arrived at the place of its desiring, it sees a lady held in reverence, splendid in light; and through her radiance the pilgrim spirit looks upon her being." To him she was Lucia, the bringer of light.

Oh, poor Lucia. She's butting in again just when I'm talking to you. She would like me to spend all my time in the afterlife with her; I do understand it, of course. She missed out on so much love on earth that she can't get enough of it now, even up here.

NINETEEN

THE ETERNAL PLAINS are bathed in a pale glow when Lucia, Daniel, Oskar and I get into our saddles for a good gallop, which doesn't keep us from continuing the discussion we've been having for several days now: should we allow others to join us?

The children of the painter Gauguin have asked to sit at our table, but Daniel and Oskar don't think they are handicapped or different enough. And then there are the many children of the philosopher Rousseau, all of whom he put into a children's home without giving them a second thought while he himself was writing his famous *Émile, ou De l'éducation*; the founding principle of educational science, expounded by a man who turned his back on his own offspring. But while they are not exactly bright, they're not quite dim enough for our taste, either; though Lucia and I don't agree on this point. Lucia says we shouldn't exclude anyone, I say we should only admit those who have been excluded the most, and before we know it, we're in the middle of a fight! Even here, in the afterlife.

Eduard Einstein, Albert's schizophrenic son, is in with a good chance. Jolting along after us as fast as his donkey will carry him, he's giving us a short summary of his life.

On earth, he was an intelligent, sensitive and, above all, highly musical boy. He studied medicine and wanted to become a psychiatrist, but was, ironically, diagnosed with schizophrenia himself when he was about twenty years old. His parents' divorce was a blow to him, and his healthy brother Hans Albert agrees that his stays in sanatoriums and foster families did him more harm than

good. The electroshock treatment he received was particularly
devastating. His father Albert and mother Mileva's relationship has
been widely commented on by the earthlings. Some believe that she
did a large part of the work which earned him his first Nobel Prize.
What is certain is that the high costs of Eduard's treatments left her
short of funds, and that his father refused to share the prize money
with her.

In 1933, Albert moved to Princeton in the United States with his
second wife, where he played the role of successful celebrity scientist
with aplomb. Eduard, who was twenty-three at the time, stayed
behind with his mother. Apart from the occasional letter, he would
hear nothing more of his father, and never see him again. After his
diagnosis, he threw himself into music and literature; he played and
composed music and wrote poetry that – though he says so himself –
was not without merit. In 1965, after staying in sanatoriums almost
continuously for two decades, he died of a stroke at the age of fifty-
five.

And now Lucia is rhapsodising about how lovely it would be if
she could dance to music that Eduard had composed specially for her.

Oh, Hagar, I'm just rattling down some of the better-known
cases, but the list of neglected children of intelligent, creative and
artistic fathers is endless. In response to Gauguin abandoning his
family to paint noble savage women on Tahiti, the philosopher
Bernard Williams even coined a term for the phenomenon: "moral
luck"; the luck of famous and successful men who leave their
children in the lurch, and get away with it, as long as they use their
reclaimed freedom to create immortal works of art for humanity.
Lucia has already stopped listening. She's waving to Eduard.

I know that on earth, they would have had children together and
the whole story would have started from the beginning: Eduard, too
sensitive – and too musical – for fatherhood would have neglected

his family, and the highly gifted Lucia would have done the same. That is why we are all glad that you can't produce children in the afterlife.

You'll think that's easy for me to say, as I was just a vegetating plant during my life on earth. My hands, which drooped like limp leaves from the snapped stems of my arms, were only ever stained with mud. I never had someone else's blood on my hands, my fingers were too weak to wield a weapon, my brain too feeble to know how to use one; I wasn't able to tell friend from foe, and my legs, unable to walk, could never stray from the straight and narrow path. I was incapable of imagining anything that could change the course of history for good or bad, and therefore unable to hatch evil schemes, reach for Olympus, develop the theory of relativity, adhere to the wrong ideologies, strive for insane purity or root out supposed ugliness. Nor was I ever in a position to abandon my children, to be too lazy or cowardly to look after them, or afraid that such devotion would undermine my own success. I'm a paragon of innocence, don't you think?

TWENTY

"THE FLOWER HAS SNAPPED!" mother Julsing cried, bowing her own head. Father Julsing joined her, then the children. They lifted me out of bed, carried me to the living room and put me down in my own little cot, which they had placed in the middle of the room so everyone could stand around it to say goodbye. My mother, in The Hague, was informed by telephone. A couple of local children came around the next day after school was out, as did Miss Nel Leys, the nanny who had looked after me for a while. This small handful of people came together again a few days later, for my quiet burial in the Old Cemetery of Gouda.

I had hoped that instead of nailing me into a coffin, they would bundle me into my pull cart and take me to the graveyard in it, just as they had constantly carted me around during my life. I loved sitting in the cart, which I relied on for most of my mobility. All the children who were big enough were allowed to take turns pulling me for a bit. Being dead, I would have liked to have used my newly acquired afterlife awareness to experience the feeling of being pulled along over the bumpy cobbles of the twisting roads, to watch the clouds glide past high above me in all their expansive serenity while I myself lay on my back as still as a corpse. I made a seamless transition from cradle to pram to pull cart to grave.

But as I was soon to notice, the wishes of the dead hold little sway with the living. All I could do was watch meekly as they fiddled and fussed over me to make me pretty enough for the viewing despite my huge head, and of course I could forget about a pull cart funeral.

In the lying position that death imposes on the body, I finally seemed to have found my natural posture. I could stop struggling against gravity, which had plagued me for so long. I didn't have to stretch my neck, heave up my head, hoist up my chin, raise my arms, stir a foot, lift a finger or say a word; I was freed from the burdens of earthly life. Lying down, my body did what came effortlessly, allowing my monstrousness to stay hidden. In death, I finally became the way I seem to have been intended in life.

The white cap, which now stayed put, gave me an angelic appearance. Perhaps my father should have seen me dead rather than living; maybe he would have been able to love me after all.

Those who preferred focusing on my defects rather than seeing my beauty, could look at my arms and the small hands they ended in, draped over the white lace blanket like flowers with broken stems. I had very large eyes, and even now they were closed, their shape was clearly distinguishable deep down in their sockets. Instead of bulging, they were now sunk back into my head.

It was the first time I saw myself. I was a spirit, seated unseen at the foot of my own cot, in the middle of my foster family. I could hear my foster siblings cry. They couldn't understand what had happened to their mascot. They had thought my bird-like shriek would always be there, suspended above the long, deep water whenever I was lowered into the Reeuwijk Lakes. Perhaps they were right. Perhaps my shriek is still there now, but they can't hear it anymore. Their wailing was unbearable. I wanted the sound of their cheerful voices ringing in my ears to be my last memory of them, a keepsake to take with me after death, because one of the only things I had ever thought or known, had ever been able to come up with in my degenerate state, was that there would always be the summer, the afternoon, their skins and the presence of the long deep water, but now I heard my foster father recite psalms with something altogether too sinister in his throat, drowning out all earlier sounds of my life, driving them away.

The whole family started to pray. They stood there as if they were no longer individuals but had merged into one dark, many-headed, mumbling creature; a kind of octopus with heads for arms. I struggled furiously against the urge to bury my face in the oh so familiar skirts of mother Julsing, where, blinded and smothered by the fabric, I would be able to see and hear as little as the dead are supposed to see and hear. Instead, I pulled myself up at her skirt and apron and looked up into my beloved foster mother's face, where I could read in her long-suffering gaze that she had resolved to regard everything with the same, constant equanimity long ago; come what may, go what will.

;

It was after yet another Sunday service during which she had not been able to take her eyes off the tall, dark-haired woman with light blue eyes sitting a few pews away from her. She had only recently joined the church; a consul's wife, the rumor went. Her beauty and mournfulness were so strangely at odds with each other that it kindled the curiosity of my as yet foster-mother-to-be, and appealed to the goodness of heart that her faith demanded of her. And so, our small family and their large one bumped into each other at a gathering of the Christian Science Church in The Hague, of which my foster mother was also a member. The church happened to be just a fifteen-minute walk from my mother's room above Mr. Schut's photography studio. She saw the short distance between church and chamber as a sign of His guidance.

My mother was there for her terminally ill daughter, my foster mother later learned. She was waiting for death or a miracle, not knowing when to expect either; it could all be over by tomorrow, or it could take years. In some cases, patients had been known to live into their twenties. The uncertainty was unbearable, a maddening conflict between bonding and detachment, hoping and letting go, believing and giving up, loving and resisting grief, suffering intensely and never showing it. This struggle was to last eight devastating years, until the case was finally settled by the capitulation of the dear little body; but in life, love and death, no one held any rights; the Lord gave and the Lord disposed, and you accepted whatever came. Despite the prayers, the psalms, the sacrifices, the devotion and the love, my health had not improved; the cure which the great founder of the movement, Mary Baker Eddy, had promised as a reward to all who were pure of heart and intentions, had not materialized.

There was so much more sin in Gouda these days, my foster mother thought. The occupying force had introduced sins through the act of invasion. Bombings, innocent deaths, betrayal, embezzlement, exploitation, theft – what did it all mean? Was it a collective punishment for shared transgressions, just like the great flood from which only Noah was spared? What was their transgression? Were the Jews the scapegoats, washed away by the Great Flood that the occupation represented, and were the others the pure of heart who would be saved? And what about the handicapped? What sins could they be capable of? Was it enough just to differ too much from God's image? Was it a literal lack of uprightness, both in body and soul? But, on the contrary, hadn't Mary Baker Eddy claimed that all people were created in God's image, and that therefore there was no such thing as disease, only an error of the mind? And Malva? Had she not actually been ill? What had the little sweetie and her mother done wrong to be made to go through life bowed down by such suffering? God worked in mysterious ways.

And then the day had arrived when their worldly paths separated again: one Sunday, after the service, she, her husband and their numerous offspring had walked one way, the pram with the misshapen four-year-old in their midst; and the mother, all alone, the other. She had looked back countless times.

Had she done the right thing by offering her help?

Following my foster mother's train of thought, I felt a momentary hesitation run down my spine like a chill, but she soon brushed her doubts aside and turned her thoughts back, with suitable empathy, to my mother, which suddenly brought me to my mother, too.

TWENTY-ONE

MY MOTHER WAS SITTING in the train; or at least, trying to sit. She did her best to keep still, to be present. She had selected an empty compartment so she could be alone and shed her tears freely, but now she kept standing up to pace up and down as far as the confined space allowed before sitting down again, laying her hands in her lap, running her fingers over her belly in a circular motion, rubbing her palms together. I tried to pull myself up at her skirt and crawl on her lap. I wanted to let her know that I was still there, was still with her, but she didn't notice me or anything I did. By contrast, I knew all her thoughts and feelings, and they were so many and hit me with such force that I had to cling to my seat so as not to topple off.

There was the window with the view of the past years. Looking through it, she had imagined the countryside as seen from the train in Java, back when her father had taken her on trips on the electric and steam-driven tramways he'd built from Tegalea through Palasari, Citeureup, Baleendah, Cankring and Ciparay to Majalaya; straight through the jungles of Java and Borneo, in the heat, the drought, the rainy season. She had seen the view as it would have looked to my father, when he accompanied his own father on the freight trains he drove through southern Chile. Their eyes had locked for the first time when he told her about it, shortly after they had met. Sparks had flown. It was part of their common roots, she had recognized the connection immediately.

Now, there was only this Dutch view. Dry, bare and barren, devoid of nature, heat and passion, it had always been the perfect backdrop for letting her mind wander to better times. For four years, these contemplations accompanied my mother's view on her monthly trips from The Hague to Gouda and back, later occasionally interrupted by the sudden noise of a war plane, an explosion. Now she was making the journey down this dead end road and back for the last time.

My mother kept thinking back to how his arm had trembled in those first weeks, when he was sleepless with lust. Sweat poured over his body, the heat that had lingered in the house all day breaking out on him. In the evening, they had been for a walk in the dark, on the unlit roads along the kampongs. He had taken her hand. They had walked to the paddy fields, and the moon had shone so brightly they could see exactly where to tread so as not to get lost.

"You're so beautiful," he had said.

Hardly an original remark, it had been effective nonetheless. He had been impressed by her height. It had fascinated him from the first time he saw her, when they met during a cocktail party at the Marine Club tennis court that he attended out of boredom. He fancied a game with her, and she thrashed him in their very first match. Tennis had never interested him, he disliked all sports, but it must have been bliss to watch her tall frame with its long limbs, sapphire eyes and endlessly large mouth dash up and down the other side of the court. A type of woman he was not yet familiar with; a *totok*, as the locals called it. Though the family had lived in Batavia for generations and she had been born there, her parents were originally Dutch. She had made her home among the ficus trees, he had landed on her territory. On her soft soil, her lap.

It wasn't long before he seized the chance one afternoon to lay down his head on it. They had sat down at the water's edge to have the picnic they had brought along, and while she was putting the food out on a cloth, he had rested his head against her shoulder for a moment, and she laughed, allowing it, so he had lain down and put his head on her lap, just like that, his legs stretched out on the ground. She felt embarrassed, awkward, and tried to hide it by carefully stroking his hair and forehead. She was a little bit like a girl, but also had something of a mother about her, he told her.

My mother recalled all the other things he had said to her, how he had rhapsodised over the charming black curls in the nape of her neck; her exceptionally well-formed nose swooping down her profile like the scroll of a violin; the lips underneath bulging like the petals of a tulip, the lower one protruding slightly though hardly so much it was a distraction, on the contrary – he found it rather endearing, an invitation to kiss her. She was, in a word, captivating; an entrancing woman with dark hair, pale skin and long, slender limbs, who had walked up to him one evening "as if simply walking into his life," as he told her later, and he had taken her hand as a matter of course and, without having exchanged a word and without letting go of her hand for an instant, had led her away from the tennis court; into a stolen evening full of promise. The wilderness around them, so overwhelming, didn't seem intended for roaming on your own; only arm in arm or, as they were at that moment, hand in hand, could you enter the way it was meant to be entered – deferentially, like a sacred space.

Slowly placing their feet on the rustling, almost ritual breathing of the leaves, they walked through the sounds and smells that gave the darkness its unfathomable dimensions. Both understood the solemnity of the event perfectly. The path lay before them, waiting for them to tread it together. To her, in her charming naivety, it was the aisle of a church leading to the altar. The blackness around them drove them closer together, limbs entwining until their bodies had already decided they belonged to one another before they themselves had even had time to think about it. Their bodies set the example, showed them how being together was done, and they were only too happy to follow suit by laughing and talking, and by kissing, which, he whispered, was actually nothing other than a silent mutual affirmation.

Had the night been the culprit? Or the jungle? Or the heat? my mother wondered. What had made her give that consent, so difficult to take back later? Had she been cheated by the setting? Or were they meant to spend the rest of their lives in it, and had they betrayed it by leaving? Would everything have been all right, would all the displacements, disproportionalities and mistakes have been canceled out by that night that was like an immense black panther? Would the nocturnal Javanese sky have cloaked them forever? And would there have been no Malva? Or would she have been born, but flawless and healthy, and would she still be alive?

I noticed how much my mother tried to push away her memories of me, quench them, stamp them out. In the refuge of her mind, she fled back to the simple and innocent first beginnings, when he washed up on her shore like some sailor, in shirt sleeves and airy linen shorts, with tanned stubbly legs and with strong shoulders to hold onto. Brisk, dapper, witty, he was leaning against a palm tree at the marina cocktail party, watching her tennis game with a roguish eye, and she started watching him watching her to make sure it was really happening, and that look emboldened him to take up position opposite her on the tennis court.

Soon, their arms went flying through the night air, and whenever she looked up she saw the sky covered in stars like an infestation of good omens. Until he walked away from her to the water's edge, and to her surprise her legs started carrying her in his direction; slowly, slowly, not too fast, not too eagerly, as if taking a stroll through the botanical gardens, she walked toward him, but in her chest, her heart was beating faster than ever before and she forced herself to take one step at the time, a slow, deliberate step with which she left all her insecurities behind.

She had noticed him at once; he was different from all the others. Different from the English, different from the Dutch, different from the natives. A difference she could not put her finger on, only study. From his first appearance at the tennis court her gaze had latched onto him, and all she had to do was follow that gaze and everything would automatically be all right, she had assumed.

There had been no need for words. He had taken her hand as if that had been completely natural, with a casualness that had caught her off guard. Overwhelmed as she was, she had made up her mind never to let him go again.

That gesture was the traitor. No, something deeper. It was the self-evidence with which the gesture was done and the things it suggested, predicted, promised: that it would extend further, into her whole life, though it seemed to her now that it had only cast a shadow over it. Had she wanted it so much that she had tried to read everything into a single gesture at a single moment, because something she had unwittingly been waiting for all her life was finally within her grasp?

Beggars can't be choosers, my mother was thinking now; a broken heart is easily mended by the soothing stroke of a warm, smooth hand, but the glue won't stick for long because it's only spittle; nothing but slime and drool, slick and sickening and so easy for the hypocrite himself to produce, but you only find out later, much later, when you realize that even during the stroll, even as you walked hand in hand, small cracks started appearing between your palms in the darkness. Only with hindsight, looking back and thinking about what went wrong, you discover them. For there had been a tree trunk they had to step over – misjudging its height in the dark, she had stubbed her foot against it and given his hand a tug;

an unnatural, rough jerk, at which she felt a response in his hand that had not reassured her, but she had only laughed, brushing her doubts away with her other hand, her free hand.

;

My mother swept her empty hand over the train window as if trying to wipe out the ghostly reflection of her face. I was hoping she would notice me, would finally see me sitting on the seat opposite, but she looked straight through me, just as she had looked through the glass a moment earlier. All she could see were the things in her mind. My mother couldn't cry; she, who had always had a good singing voice, couldn't make a sound. And I, who had always been able to sing, the only thing I'd ever been able to do, was equally struck dumb. She because of the lump in her throat, I because the dead are stripped of their voice. We sat facing each other like two mutes, and the thought struck me that I was her shadow. All I could do now was repeat what she had become, mirror everything she did the moment she did it.

I became ice. I became a black square. I became a Javanese sword. Then I turned into the coldness of the ice, the blackness of the square, the sharpness of the sword, and finally found myself in my mother's belly, which was black and cold and seemingly stabbed. I lifted myself up to the place where her heart was still pumping, pumping away, where there was still movement, and warmth; and focusing on that, I listened to the beating that carried on as always, in spite of everything.

;

At last we arrived at Gouda station. My mother stood, hoisting herself up, swaying on leaden legs. She staggered over the road along the railway until she reached the house, knocked on the door, her fist almost too weak to make a sound, but the door was open and she walked in saying nothing, greeting no one, her eyes immediately falling on the small bed in the middle of the room, and the moment she saw it, she froze. I saw her lips move, but no words came out. I saw them tremble. I saw the tears well up in her eyes and finally fall.

;

She understood that the last words wasted on me would be the ones on my tombstone. She ordered my grave to be made in the East Indian style, the only East Indian grave in the Old Gouda Cemetery. It was lined with white tiles, and there was an upright headstone on which my name was misspelled: the local stonemason had changed the "y" in the Spanish name Reyes into the Dutch diphthong "ij" without the dots.

Not good enough for her child, the unjustly forgotten daughter of a poet, she decided. She went back to the stonemason's, her tall figure making an impression on his adolescent son that was as indelible as the letters incorrectly chiseled into the headstone. An old man now, he was just a boy at the time; but even seventy years later he remembers how she awakened his first feelings of lust as she walked into his father's masonry workshop; so tall, so dark, so elegant it gave him goose bumps.

They heard footsteps. The door of the mason's opened. Emerging from the mist of stone dust, her tall figure appeared and approached them slowly, the grievous expression on her face only gradually becoming visible. Mater dolorosa, worthy of being carved on a tombstone. His father did not like to disappoint her, but the stone was indomitable. Pietà.

She had seemed as strong as that stone, but the war and my father's dwindling financial support had left her destitute; and though she had written, begging him to send the agreed amount each month, it kept getting smaller until it had hardly been enough to safeguard my place with my foster family, had barely sufficed for the train fare to visit me once a month, was too little now to have my name carved correctly on a new headstone – so she had to resign herself to leaving it as it was.

After my death, she begged my father to get her out of the Netherlands. Her plea fell on deaf ears, and she was deported to the transit camp Westerbork as a result. The Nazi authorities, just as much in the dark about the fact that my father had already divorced her as she was, considered her Chilean because of her marriage. That foreign nationality alone was offense enough to send her to Westerbork. From Westerbork she was to be taken to Liebenau, where she was to serve as an exchange prisoner for a captured German soldier. She had hoped to travel from Liebenau to Switzerland, still deluding herself that she would be reunited with my father, whom she continued to regard as her husband. In her last month at Westerbork, the inmates already knew they would soon be freed, but liberty did not bring with it the hoped-for reunion with my father. He issued an official statement that he did not wish Maruca to leave the country, though he did not inform her of the fact, sending it only to the ambassadors and officials charged with arranging her emigration. Only much later, she found out that he had divorced her in Mexico to marry Delia, shortly before my death. Her own mother, her only living next of kin, was killed four months later in the Japanese prisoner of war camp Tjideng.

She paid for my burial rights out of her meager wages, in three installments. Twenty-two years later, following a painful illness, she was buried in an unmarked grave in The Hague, a grave that has long been cleared. Three months after her death, in June 1965, the following letter was delivered to my father's ocean-view house near the port of Valparaíso:

Dear Mr. Neruda,

A considerable time ago, we informed you by telegram of the demise of your former wife, Mrs. M. A. Reyes-Hagenaar. We hereby offer you our condolences.

We have been obliged to postpone writing the letter promised in the telegram until we were able to get a clear view of Mrs. Reyes-Hagenaar's situation (financial and otherwise), which was further complicated by the fact that in her final years, she had hardly any contact with family members or acquaintances. Please accept our apologies for the delay.

Before her passing, Mrs. Reyes-Hagenaar was ill for several months. She suffered from cancer, and although she was initially expected to make a recovery after what appeared to be a successful operation, she died fairly suddenly after a relapse. Fortunately, the loneliness of her final months was alleviated somewhat by the occasional visits of a friend.

The few possessions she left behind have been used by us to meet the costs of her burial, the due rent and so forth (several articles of clothing, bags, etc., and pieces of furniture have been sold off for this purpose). Though this will probably suffice to cover the costs, we would appreciate it if you could let us know whether you are prepared to refund certain additional outlays we may have incurred (i.e., such as have not been covered).

Furthermore, a ring and a wristwatch that belonged to Mrs. Reyes-Hagenaar are currently in our possession – if you wish, we will be happy to send them to you.

We hope the above is satisfactory to you and remain

Sincerely yours,

Mr. Van Basten

On behalf of the Hague District of the Church of Jesus Christ of Latter-day Saints.

My father received the letter with the news, written in Dutch, at his house in La Sebastiana, Valparaíso. His gaze lingered for an instant every time it encountered my mother's name – still Reyes-Hagenaar, he would think; she used the name "Reyes" until the end, as if the divorce hadn't been a fait accompli for many years.

;

I myself lived on invisibly after my death until, as if by miracle, my grave in the Old Gouda Cemetery was discovered in the centenary year of my father's birth. It was due to be cleared when the burial rights expired in 2003, but the cemetery was granted landmark status shortly before and my grave was left intact. And while Antonio Reynaldos, a Chilean who had fled to the Netherlands, was still looking for it, the Dutch translator of Matilde's memoirs, Giny Klatser, discovered the grave she recognized as the tomb of the only daughter of the great Chilean poet who had written in his memoirs:

"When I die, I want to be buried in a name, some specially chosen, beautiful-sounding name, so that its syllables will sing over my bones, near the sea."

;

In Isla Negra, the sound of the sea is already starting to sing the syllables of my name. I can hear it. My father hears it too. He will wake up one morning, and everything I have written above will suddenly prove untrue. The suppression of my memory wiped out by one lash of the sea's whip.

He'll say to Matilde, "I had a dream last night. The sea was calling out my daughter's name. The roaring of the waves kept repeating the word *Malva, Malva, Malva,* very slowly, calmly, and I stood on the shore, looked out over the endless surge as if this were all the water of the earth, of all the tears, of all hydrocephalic heads, and I thought to myself: what a hackneyed dream I'm having, just as well I didn't write this. Then I woke up."

;

The next night, my father's sleep is undisturbed. The sea does not sing my name again. It only calls out its own: *Mar, Mar, Mar* (I was mistaken, I heard Malva but it was "Mar"), the sea, the sea, the seaaaaaa. *¡Sólo la mar! Padre ¿por qué me trajiste acá?*, I hear the late Rafael Alberti, a friend of my father's, whisper somewhere in my afterlife.

TWENTY-TWO

I REMEMBER HOW I DIED. I was lying in bed, covered by a cotton sheet and a woollen blanket. "Sleep tight, sweet flower," mother Julsing had just said to me. Suddenly, the room was filled with wailing sirens and the loud drone of war planes above the house, which lay beside the Gouda railway line. The noise had been familiar to me ever since hearing the bullets whistling past the Barcelona hotel where Mom and I were hiding at the beginning of the Civil War.

It also reminded me of Federico. He appeared in my mind's eye, standing at my cradle in Madrid. While others bending over me to take a closer look at this newborn girl, the child of the great poet Neruda, recoiled in horror at seeing my unappetizing head stick out from under the sheets, Federico, and he was almost the only one ever to do this, bent even lower and whispered a few words into my ear.

In between the noises of war, my room was completely silent. I concentrated on the memory of the melodious lilt of Federico's voice. While the expanding water reservoir in my head was relentlessly pushing out and cutting off ever more brain functions, those parts enabling me to hear and recognize tunes and sounds remained astonishingly unimpaired. And so I heard Federico's voice in my mind's ear again, uttering the exact words he had written specially for me at my birth in Madrid in 1934. The voice in my head died away, until, at the last, whispered line, I had already fallen into that deep sleep.

Lines written on the birth of Malva Marina Neruda

Dearest Malva, I wonder will you ever
waltz the endless waves, a dolphin abroad
past the poison, past the pain
of your Americas' mortal dove.

And can I halt the howling night
Its hooves advancing down the hills,
will we ever withstand the colossal wind
the daisy cutter that turns us all to shade.

The White Elephant at your side can't tell
whether to give you a rose or a sword
from your Javanese green hands or the iron flames,
from the Chilean sea; the waltzes, the wreaths.

My sweetheart in Madrid, Malva Marina,
I'll not cover you in flowers and shells
but spread with love across your lips
this blossom of salt for the celestial light.

It is true. I do look like a dolphin; a mammal that, like me, has a highly pronounced forehead, a bulge just above its eyes. It hadn't escaped Federico's attention that my father and mother had pursued each other by the sea, in Java, where my mother had lived her whole life when my father appeared like a star on her firmament.

They both came from different faraway climes which nevertheless had a lot in common: Java and Chile, long strips of land bordering on the sea, veined by rivers, charred by volcanic eruptions, lashed by rains; the warm tropical downpours in the Java of my mother and the cool Araucan drizzle in the southern Chile of my father. The countryside was lavish, capricious and ungovernable, very different from little Gouda, which, though the "wettest city in the Netherlands," was another kind of wet altogether. "And can I halt the howling night / Its hooves advancing down the hills," Federico wrote for me, and of course he meant that the disaster looming over me should be averted, the fate that had befallen the Neruda family staved off, and good things brought back. The mortal dove was of course man, from whom blood and poison is drawn, which would explain why he's lying in that crooked position.

The White Elephant is probably the cuddly soft toy placed next to a cot to guard over it, bring the baby gifts and ponder about which ones. He has to choose from all the best things the ancestral countries of the newborn can offer – a sword from Java or a floral wreath from Chile – but, being a wise elephant, the White Elephant decides differently. A sword or a rose would have been appropriate gifts on the birth of a normal girl: a sword for fighting and a rose for loving, just as everyone has to fight and love in turn; has to fight in order to love. But as the sensitive Federico realized from the beginning, I needed more powerful attributes to make my existence on earth halfway bearable – after all, someone with a waterlogged brain wielding a sword can fight only windmills, as the true enemy lurks inside their head, the one thing they cannot fight. Chop it off, and you lose everything else with it.

And the rose, of what use would that be for someone as hideous as me, so repulsive that no one would ever seek my hand, no one ever want to steal my heart? Not even a rose garden could have made that happen, for while a crowning rose enhances beauty, on ugliness it's like a sprig of parsely on a dog's dinner. So the sensible, sensitive Federico, who knew and foresaw everything intuitively, gave me a different gift. Something of more use to me in my pitiful state. He gave me salt.

According to a Latin American folklore, salt allows you to live on after death, and that is exactly what happened to me. Even though there was no real salt involved, only the salt that Federico García Lorca imagined putting to my lips at my birth in his poem, it was nevertheless that salt that gave me eternal life after death. It is the reason why I can tell my story at all, why I can talk about it in such detail.

Where I am now, in the realm of immortal ghosts, I've also heard whispered rumors that I have my Latin American blood to thank for being admitted to this afterparty of the dead. After all, Latinos are familiar with the concept of people living on after death. María Luisa Bombal, a good friend of both my father and my mother, wrote about it in *The Shrouded Woman*. Sitting at my parents' kitchen table in Buenos Aires, María Luisa wrote: "Perhaps people are like plants, not all are called to blossom, and some even grow on desert plains without water because they lack hungry roots."

She also wrote: "And who knows, perhaps not every death is the same. Perhaps we each take a different path after death."

In *The House of the Spirits*, Isabel Allende quotes these lines of my father's poetry as an epigraph to her book:

How much does a man live, after all?
Does he live a thousand days, or one only?
For a week, or for several centuries?
How long does a man spend dying?
What does it mean to say "forever"?

"Every people get the afterlife it deserves for its literature," claim some of those I try to spend the afterlife with in as pleasant as possible a manner, but that's a load of chauvinist drivel, if you ask me – unfortunately, that doesn't end with death, either. Personally, I believe that my stay in the afterlife is entirely and exclusively down to Federico's salt. And the others must owe their continued existence to some other line of verse, by some other poet.

My thoughts falter when I think of the beautiful young poet Miguel Hernández, the goat herder who often took me for walks in the park in my pram to give my mother some breathing space. Having lost his own first child a few months after birth, Miguel was hoping to avert another such tragedy by finding the best specialists for me and letting me spend a holiday on the coast with his own parents, where I was to grow stronger under the powerful Spanish sun, but then a civil war broke out. Federico was shot dead in a valley near Viznar, close to his native village, and Miguel was arrested shortly afterwards. He was visiting his wife, who had just given birth to their second child, and he wanted desperately to be with her. Years later, he died from tuberculosis in a cold dungeon without ever having seen his little son again.

I suddenly realize with a shock that the two dearest poets, the only ones who were ever good to me, were also the ones to risk, and lose, their lives by putting their families first – while my father, who abandoned his family, went on living. The nicest people usually die first in a war. I sometimes think that this was my mother's greatest fault; she was simply too kindhearted. But I digress. I was telling you about the moment of my death.

Just before I died that evening, I imagined a blossom of salt and love and celestial light lying on my mouth, and licking my lips, I pretended to suck on all these physical and metaphysical things.

I have now found that love, and the celestial light is falling on me as I speak these words.

TWENTY-THREE

"THE SPRING BEGINS with a great yellow labor. Everything is covered in countless tiny golden flowers. The small but powerful germination coats the hillsides, girdles rocks, stretches out to sea and appears in the middle of the paths we walk over daily, as if challenging us, as if trying to prove its existence to us. The flowers have led a hidden existence for so long, in the desolate denial of the sterile soil, that nothing seems good enough for their yellow profusion now.

[...] The farmers and fishermen of my country have long since forgotten the names of the plants and flowers. And with their gradual forgetting, the flowers slowly lost their pride. They became overgrown and obscured, like the stones that the rivers carry from the snow of the Andes to unknown shores. Farmers and fishermen, miners and smugglers aren't concerned with anything but their own bitterness, the constant death and revival of their duties, their defeats. There is little glory in being the hero of as yet unexplored territories; the truth is that in them and in their songs, nothing shines but the most anonymous of blood, and the flowers whose name nobody knows."

He puts down his pen. I watch the green ink on the paper lose its gloss as it dries. The letters look a bit like small plants.

A few moments ago, I saw the abundance of flowers he conjured up in his mind, and which simultaneously unfolded like a fan before my eyes, in the wild. I awoke on the coast of Isla Negra in Chile, stirred by the thunder of Pacific Ocean waves crashing onto the beach nearby.

As he writes, the flowers pop up before my eyes, written flowers on a written coast that is nevertheless real. I have never seen the world in all its violent fury from this close before. For a moment, I think I'm in paradise, when in fact this is just what the real world is like, and I realize for the first time how barren the earth was that I inhabited on earth itself. Here, everything is pregnant, budding, full of hope, in the making. Nature has passed through my father's thoughts and into his words.

So this is my father in his natural habitat.

So this is where he is now, my father.

A black back, shoulders, head, all silhouette, are outlined against the glaring light that falls in through the window.

I approach his figure from behind, like an intruder, a prowler, though I don't mean him any harm. I've come here to meet my father.

But when I spot the lines he has written, I decide to steal them. I nick the versions he discarded, the words he declined. Like a bird pecking worms and small fish, I pick letters out of his sentences. Or, more accurately, since these are rejected words and discarded sentences, I'm eating carrion, word carrion and letter carrion, sentence carrion, scrumptious – I munch and crunch this lunch of language into words of my own. He doesn't notice a thing.

This is where I like being most, in the salty sea air of Isla Negra, lying on the warm sand in the broiling afternoon silence, brooding on words in the breeze that sways the flowers, or in the buzz of a bumblebee.

I tolerate her, the "She" in his life. First Delia, the Carillon. Her dingdong is growing fainter already. This is where she turns sixty, seventy, finally settles into the peace of the coast in spite of herself until, head held high, she disappears from my father's riotous life to paint her magnificent horses. Then comes his last wife, Matilde; la Patoja. Small hands digging and grubbing around in the soil. Dainty feet strolling around the garden surrounding the house, where she cultivates that which flourishes and flowers in abundance elsewhere.

The same hands cultivate him, too; regularly pruning his nails and hair, preparing his food and doing his accounts. She is a small, nimble, lively spirit bustling busily about the house and garden all day.

I follow her around for days on end. But, as I know, there's something missing.

That something almost arrived one day. They had already chosen his name. When she miscarried at three months, my father thought she had not looked after herself and blamed her for the loss, as she wrote in her memoirs, just as he had held my deformity against my mother.

What a terrible, terrible shame that I can't be born a second time here.

TWENTY-FOUR

EVENINGS AT ISLA NEGRA. The ocean pounds the beach. The sea blends seamlessly into the night. The house is brightly lit. There are candles in the windows. My father and Delia are awake. My father and Matilde are asleep. I swing from a beam. I loiter in a shaft. The house is my castle. I whirl out of a crack. I disappear in a corner, ride on my father's large brown cardboard horse or, chuff chuff, in the old train engine in the garden that reminds my father of Walt Whitman, the steam that used to come out of its chimney being Whitman's white beard. Every morning, I mutter to the sea shells, the figureheads, Chuff Chuff the big engine with its Windblown Beard, and the horse, "In the morning, Malva salutes the things."

I don't play with the things themselves, I play with their souls, but not their actual souls, as things don't have any; I play with the souls my father gave his things in his poems. The souls he gave them are as alive as I am. Everything he composed is as alive as I am now, after my death – this is the world he has given me posthumously and which I am part of, here, on this side of the paper, on this side of reality.

;

My thoughts are swirling along with the autumn leaves. Always the sound of my own voice. That's what being dead is like. Hearing only your own voice and unable to make it heard; like being buried in your own head. I want to borrow a hand that can express what I think, write it down. My father won't do it; he washed his hands of me a long time ago. I need a different hand, a hand that won't recoil from me. Please, Hagar, can it be yours?

;

Do I ever catch my father thinking of me on earth? Not once! My banishment is complete. He sleeps well, untroubled by the slightest pangs of conscience. I watch him closely in those early days, observing this; to make absolutely sure it is really the case, that it is possible he has shut me out completely. How can that be, you ask?

One day, walking through a meadow of wildflowers – the mallow he knows from the coast – he catches, for an instant, like an echo reverberating in the chamber of his mind only because of its sound and lasting a second at most, the fragment of a memory. It is not a memory of my existence, nor of my birth, illness or death; more like the last throes of a time in which that sound was still a distant hope, before even this Malva materialized, the Malva he identifies the flowers with. The Malva I could have been, I should have become – she is who the flowers remind him of.

;

Going through my father's bookshelves one morning, I encounter *Malva*, the story by Gorky, in a book given to him as an adolescent by Gabriela Mistral. The Chilean poet who would later be awarded the Nobel Prize was his school teacher in Temuco at the beginning of his literary education, when he read all the great Russians.

And there they are: the girl Malva and the sea. She's pretty, this

Malva, very pretty. Her smile reveals pearly white teeth, she has full breasts, an hour-glass figure and tanned, muscular legs. Is this the moment, while reading this story as a seventeen-year-old, that the name Malva entered his head? Did the thought cross his mind: *later, if I ever have a daughter –*

Now I stand face to face with her, the Malva I could never be. I run to her father Gorky, ask him, "Are we alike? Is this me?" He nods politely, for he loves hard-pressed women and I am without a doubt the hardest-pressed of them all.

"Yes," he says decidedly, banging his fist on the table. "Yes. You are the Malva I envisaged in my novella! I can see the beauty of your soul, just like hers, I can see the strength of your ambition, the power of your will to never give up. What does your condition say about you, what does her poverty say about a farmer's wife? What do his circumstances say about the soul of a man? What do they say about his conscience? His inner dignity? Nothing! Nothing! You are even more beautiful than the Malva I painted with my pen, I was so young, forgive me my shallowness, forgive me for lusting after my own creation. I should have modeled her after you. Oh, if I were still alive, if Stalin, to whom your father is now writing his declarations of love, hadn't poisoned me, I would write a new *Malva*, my dearest *Petrushka*. And I will, here in the afterlife, I'll make a new *Malva* for you, I promise. Come back later, at regular intervals, and sit down on the chair you're sitting on now. I'll read her to you, from start to finish, my beautiful Malva. Go now, and be at peace and rest. Don't torture yourself, you exquisite being."

And bravely, that is, without hesitation, he plants a kiss on my deformed head.

;

On warm afternoons, I accompany my father and Delia or Matilde, whichever of the two is present, on blissful strolls along the seashore, searching both their hands, listening to his words to her and pretending they were addressed to me.

"Nuptial fruit, sweetheart?"

"Yes, Daddy."

And their evenings in the domestic comfort of each other's company in the living room, he writing, she reading:

"Darling, I'm going to bed. Will you switch off the light?"

"You go on ahead little Ant, my little Shorty, I'll be up in a moment."

My longing for my father is rapidly turning into a form of self-torment, which I have to admit to secretly enjoying – so much so I'm not sure which attachment is stronger: that to my misfortune or that to him. As a man, he is actually quite interchangeable. I can't say I love him, since I've never really known him. It doesn't matter anymore. Immediately after my death, I became obsessed with undoing his rejection of me. I will reach him, no matter what; whatever it takes, I will make him accept me.

And I slip in between his model boats and old seashells, his Manrique, his Góngora, his Garcilaso, his Quevedo, his Lautréamont and his Mayakovsky, playing hide and seek.

TWENTY-FIVE

AFTERNOONS IN VALPARAÍSO. The harbor down below, the hills above dotted with houses, the view of the old city and the sea. The narrow, steep lanes terracing the slopes, and then more sea, the endless ocean.

In the long afternoons he spends writing, I sometimes wriggle in between his torso and the table and settle on his lap. I descend like a leaf in the fall, a falling sheet of paper he has flung over his shoulder without first scrunching it up into a ball; the wrong version. As he bends over another blank sheet, a tabula rasa, his pen poised, I leap on top of him. His arm goes straight through my body, but that doesn't deter me. I pretend he is hugging me, that his writing hand is stroking me, his child on his lap.

I hover over the paper, watching his hand holding the pen move from left to right and the letters appear in green ink.

Timidly, I whisper in his ear, "Don't do that, not that word, not 'root' again, you've used it so often already. Just look at the lines above," but he brushes my advice aside and the word "root" remains ineradicable. I hear his deep breathing behind me, a steady noise as tranquil as calm water, at peace and deeply connected with all things. His calm calms me. I close my eyes and imagine all is well.

;

They crop up everywhere, the roots, origins and causes, as if he were willing his words to take root, to anchor his feet firmly to the ground which so often fell from under them as a result of his mother's death and his endless travels, while constellations of entourages danced around him like crystals, taking each other's place like secret lovers, or wives. His best friends were snatched away from him by the brutal hands of their murderers, and he waved goodbye to his daughter (defenseless, lost, given up at birth by the doctors unless her disorder resolved itself spontaneously, which had been known to happen, you could never tell beforehand) when she was two years old, and never gave her a backward glance. But I'm waving back. Just watch me wave.

Waving, not drowning.

;

Sometimes, I return to my hoped-for afterlife grandmother, Szymborska. I'm going to wear her down until the day I hear my own suggestion coming from her lips! Just as intent on finding my roots and my origin, I won't stop badgering her and asking her questions until I will have defined myself. If anyone knows who I am, she does.

Since she won't allow me to be a mermaid, fawn or angel, I ask Szymborska whether she thinks I could pass myself off as a tarsier instead. The tarsier does live on earth, and, as the Polish poet wrote in the sublunary world, we are glad it exists because its complete uselessness is a comfort to us. Keen to claim for myself the characteristics she attributed to the exemplary little creatures, I repeat them in her own words:

"And only we few who remain unstripped of fur,
untorn from bone, unplucked of soaring feathers,

esteemed in all our quills, scales, tusks, and horns,
and in whatever else that ingenious protein
has seen fit to clothe us with,
we, my lord, are your dream,
which finds you innocent for now.

[...]

a tiny creature, nearly half of something,
yet nonetheless, a whole no less than others,
so light that twigs spring up beneath my weight
and might have lifted me to heaven long ago
if I hadn't had to fall
time and again
like a stone lifted from hearts
grown oh so sentimental:
I, a tarsier,
know well how essential it is to be a tarsier."

"But you are *not* a tarsier." Szymborska interrupts me, shattering
my illusion with her pragmatic remark. "Tarsiers are useless and
superfluous, but they are not misshapen, or a burden. You are not
a 'whole no less than others.' After all, you are not whole, and you
are inferior to others, which is why you died young. You were meant
to be different from what you eventually became. The tarsier wasn't.
I'm sorry, I really do not begrudge you anything, but I want to see
the world with honest, unprejudiced eyes. We have no choice but to
view your former presence on earth in a different light."

Szymborska continues to sing the praises of conservative
Mother Nature. Mother Nature is conservative out of necessity –
who knows what kinds of monsters would emerge otherwise – and

then of course there is natural selection, which exists for good reason and is more intelligent than we, former earthly mortals, can fathom. We mortals would be on the brink of extinction if certain standards weren't upheld, and we should be grateful to her, Mother Nature, for the occasional excesses she does permit herself, within the boundaries of what is possible:

> "And after all she does permit a fish to fly,
> deft and defiant. Each such ascent
> consoles our rule-bound world,"

"While my dying of my huge head weighs it down," I interrupt my hoped-for grandmother, but she goes on stubbornly:

> "reprieves it
> from necessity's confines – more
> than enough for the world to be a world."

"But surely, the world is still a world with me in it?" I ask, just as stubborn. "Even if my presence devalues it. I tamper with the finely wrought clockwork, I fiddle with God's creation. I know perfectly well I wasn't meant like this; I am the jeer of creation, the price that must be paid for so much beauty, so much perfection, the exception that proves the rule; but still just as necessary as the tarsier, precisely because of my superfluousness. I am that which everyone would rather forget, and that is exactly what I am here to remind them of: the possibility of something going wrong. I am the embodiment of error, a mistake on legs, a walking blunder of Mother Nature.

"Actually, even walking is too much to be asked, I don't function well enough for that. Not that I'm broken; I was never whole. I never reached completion, maturity. But here, I'm as nimble as a cat; I can catch my father's inspirations before he can put them to paper. I listen to his thoughts, that amorphous mass of brewing ideas swirling through his mind, just as I used to listen to the music I heard in my mother's uterine tower, peacefully floating around before my birth: the muted hum coming from a distant open space I sensed all around me. I witness the incubation of a brain wave, and the speed with which he coaxes it to maturity. Every day, hundreds of words are born to my father."

;

Szymborska nods, and pointing to earth, where my father is writing unsuspectingly, she continues her cool hymn to Mother Nature undaunted:

"And after all she does permit us baroque gems
like this: a platypus that feeds its chicks on milk.
She might have said no – and which of us would know
that we'd been robbed?
                              But the best is that
she somehow missed the moment when a mammal turned up
with its hand miraculously feathered by a fountain pen."

Reciting the final three lines, she looks at me triumphantly. She must think she is doing me a favor by referring to my father, or if not my father then at least someone of his species, the family of mammals whose hand is feathered by a fountain pen; the archetype of the writer and, in her view, the pinnacle of creation.

"Go ahead, rub it in!" I whisper in a choked voice. "Rub salt in the wound – much as I love the stuff –, it hurts! My father was such a mammal. He, too, had taken up and worn the gauntlet that

Nature had thrown down, complete with the beautifully fountain-pen-feathered hand, and in its ink, penned a fate that was denied to me in the eight years of my meager existence. On paper, he molded reality to his will, adding fawns, angels and goodness knows what other fabrications, while I struggled to get a grip on everyday reality. While my impairments didn't allow me to lead a normal existence, he was given not just an ordinary life – and an extremely pleasant one, too – but also his imagination and the rewards he reaped from it in the form of fulfilment, fame and wealth.

"Sometimes, my father's well-fed, wonderfully fountain-pen-feathered hand brushes over the green ink of the lines he just wrote. If only I could be those lines, I think, watching; stroke my papyrus, my parchment, my translucent face, my light, my darkness – come on, father, stroke me like you caress everything else you have brought forth. You even look tenderly at the writing you mark for improvement. You treat poems you reject at first reading with the indulgence you'd show a child with much to learn. You have always given them a second chance, wrapped them up in new versions. 'Why can't I be revised?' I ask him. 'For as long as it takes for me to meet your expectations, for you to mutter contentedly, "done!" Why won't you do that for me? Why is flesh rigid as rock, why can't tissue be bent – does skin not flow like water, are bones not made of air? Why, father? Just look at me; mine are, my bones are made of air. Up here, my skin flows like an invisible current all around you, murmuring just like your breath, but you don't notice.' It's not fair!" I accidentally shout the words that were meant for my father at Szymborska. "How I would have wanted to take up the gauntlet with the pen attached, but it wasn't thrown down for me! And even if it had been tossed my way, I wouldn't have been able to pick it up as my hands didn't have the strength to do so. Nor could I have drawn a weapon and crossed swords with him, however much I wanted to fight him, however much I wished Federico had given me the Javanese dagger at my birth – and now, in death, I know what to do: I take up the gauntlet, the hand armed with the fountain pen that is also a sword, and I fight, here and now, word for word; letter for letter; punctuation mark for punctuation mark; period for comma for comma for period; preparing my father's demise after he concealed mine. Blood and ink are thicker than water, father, and look: here they flow. In jet-black letters that crawl like scorpions."

The afterlife resounds with the call of my gaaaaaaaaaaaaaaaaaaaaaall.

Szymborska, in her infinite wisdom, only looks me in the eye, a deep, long look, then shakes her head and disappears like an angel in the night.

TWENTY-SIX

I CAN HEAR MY FATHER'S nasal, sonorous voice in the background. He's reciting a poem he just finished to Matilde, to hear what it sounds like out loud. He dictates, she types.

The sound comes from far off, from a different room than the one I'm playing in. I'm lying under the table with my ear to the floor. The four words I catch are enough for me to recognize the poem he's writing, and without interrupting my game, I quietly mumble the lines to myself, correcting them as I go along, but he, far away in the other room, doesn't hear me, and our versions start diverging, differing from each other. My version is finished while I can still hear him talking, on and on, meandering around a single topic; a sound coming from far off like the sea at Isla Negra washing onto the shore and rushing out again, and there is something so calming and comforting about it that it sends me, a dead person, to sleep.

When I wake up, everything is dark and quiet. The house seems deserted. In the pale light, I see the shadows of the figureheads that are staring at me with large eyes. The same pale light illuminates the glass bottles on the windowsill, showing the outlines of ship models inside. My father and Matilde have gone to sleep a long time ago. The only sound comes from the sea.

I get up from the floor and sneak upstairs to take a look in their bedroom. There he lies: large, stocky and content, his arms flung generously around her narrow shoulders. She, asleep on his chest, her face and closed eyes even paler in the moonlight. They themselves have become figureheads of the ship of the night, their bodies outposts of their dreams, their faces painted like masks to ward off evil spirits. Their two intertwined frames form an entity that excludes me, that shuts me out of the pool of moonlight falling at my feet. Living, breathing in unison like this, they join forces in their nocturnal embrace to drive me, their demon, away.

If I look at the body of my father's third wife very closely, I can see the outlines of Delia through it. The bedroom changes with her, taking on the appearance of a different room of the house, the one he shared with Delia. And if I keep looking, I can even see the figure of my mother, many years earlier. The outlines of the womens' bodies blend into each other at first, as if painted with the light falling in through the windows of the church in Gouda, whose shades of color I so often used to watch flow into each other when I squinted my eyes in a certain way. Now, I keep them wide open. I see the bodies of the later women gradually fade as the figure of my mother becomes clearer, until the latter has completely replaced the other two.

My father is much younger. The background noise is no longer the stormy surge of the Pacific at Isla Negra, but the rippling of the Indian Ocean. Now we are in Java, its clammy heat, its own silences and smells. The embrace itself is less intimate; there is as yet none of the casualness entrenched by years of sleeping in this position, and, as I can sense very clearly, there is also less affection.

I focus my gaze to yet another time, even earlier, on one of their first nights. My father's arm is trembling, he is sleepless with lust.

I feel a short-lived impulse to appear before their eyes, undo their embrace and lie down between them, imagining their bewilderment as they grope my distorted form in their sleep, trying to determine whether what they are feeling is true. Running their fingers over my bulging skull in a rising panic. Finally waking up with a start, having realized I'm not the other lying next to them; hoping it is only a nightmare.

TWENTY-SEVEN

AFTER I DIED, MY MOTHER was left wading through a fog that never lifted. The Hague in wartime was even more forbidding than it had been before. My mother hoped for an explosion nearby, she hoped for death. Every day when the curfew bell rang she hid away in the darkness of her room, blankets pulled over her head. Then she would trace her life's story back in her mind, always returning to the point where she had taken the wrong turn, after which one step inescapably followed the other, leading her here, to The Hague, in the war year 1943, on the first floor, in bed, alone, in the pitch dark.

I don't really have the nerve to go inside; into the room where my mother is slowly breaking apart.

During the day, the ground floor of the photographer who rented her the room was full of the clients having their pictures taken for the identity cards that were about to be made obligatory. An advertisement had appeared in the papers:

ACT NOW BEFORE IT IS TOO LATE!
HAVE YOUR IDENTITY CARD PHOTOGRAPH TAKEN
AT SCHUT PHOTOGRAPHY,
GROOT HERTOGINNELAAN 209
IN THE HAGUE.

IDENTITY CARDS WILL SHORTLY BE COMPULSORY.
THE PHOTOGRAPHS MEET ALL SPECIFICATIONS
OF THE REQUIREMENTS COMMITTEES.

When I was staying with the Julsing family, I was far too young to have my picture taken, as identity cards were only obligatory for children over the age of twelve. Otherwise, I would have made a train journey to The Hague with my mother and would have posed in the studio below her rental room; I would have enjoyed my afternoon nap in her bed, just like in the old days, in the time before our separation. I would have passed the purple-pink orchids standing in the ornamental window bars in the hall, and my mother would have pointed them out to me with her beautiful, slender fingers.

"Look, Malva: mauve flowers – as mauve as the mallow, the flower you were named after!"

And though I would have understood nothing of what she said, I'd have admired the flowers' slim stems and striking colors. I would have been carried up the mysterious staircase, marveling at the strange smells, the dimness, the deep yellow shadows, the golden glow, and I would have seen the dusty light in the space above me sparkle like a starry sky in broad daylight. Afterwards, back with my foster family in Gouda, I would undoubtedly have felt homesick for that hidden Hague territory of my mother's.

Visiting her later, after my death, I realized those were the memories I had been denied; my mother's room, which I had never actually seen. I crept up the stairs without disturbing a single, dancing speck of dust on the communal landings; nothing leapt up, nothing flew about, and besides the occasional door standing ajar, a curtain billowing in the wind and flapping against a window, the place was as quiet as the grave. As if these were homes of the dead, as if everyone in them had already become a spirit.

But I realize I'm still stalling.

;

Standing at the window, my mother watches them come and go, the identifiable, those about to be weighed in the balance and found either satisfactory or wanting, on the basis of the race they happen to belong to, on the basis of something they were born with, without ever having been given a choice.

"Life is harsh," my mother thinks, watching the approach of fresh customers for Schut without knowing yet that she herself, thanks to that identity card, will have to spend a month in camp Westerbork at the end of the war because of her marriage to my foreign father. "You come into the world, are born into a body with no idea which, what, where and how – circumstances just take shape around you, close in on you like a web while all the time you think it will be all right, that everything is as it should be because here you are, born to a mother and father just like everyone else, until one day you suddenly find that the circumstances have taken a different turn without any consideration for you, that new criteria apply, the rules have changed, and you are told by the powers that be that you no longer meet requirements; and suddenly it is too late to escape.

"It all happens very gradually. At first, you don't take much notice of the changes in the way they treat you, unaware of what is happening around you. You're trustworthy, a trusting soul, the way you were brought up to be. But somewhere, in a place you have no access to, the cards are reshuffled and a die is cast, and the rules about their symbols, their size, their nature, their numbers, are quietly changed. Next thing you know, you've been sidelined, powerless to object. All ears you appeal to are deaf to everything but those new rules, made by others. They won't listen to all your reasonable arguments, shutting out first your love, then your complaints and objections, until finally you become too much of a nuisance for not adapting to the new world order and they start looking for ways of getting rid of you. Preferably as quietly as possible, with the least possible amount of fuss and commotion. No need to advertize the fact that they are violating the rights of humanity and love. They don't like to be reminded of it either. They prefer preserving their good opinion of themselves. After all, they need to spend the rest of their lives with themselves, so it's only natural they want to be able to look into the mirror in the morning. And so they'll make it look like you have only yourself to blame for this failure, this humiliation, this betrayal."

Sitting on the bed, I shift closer to my mother and put my arms around her. She doesn't notice, I don't give off any body heat. Thinking the same thoughts as she does, I try channeling them off at a certain point, try stemming their flow with my own, but can't think of the right words. I can't delude her with a different reality, and in the end, I too am gripped by the current of my mother's thoughts and washed away with it. I surrender to its course and wait until it is all over, her tears have dried up and we have both fallen asleep. She sleeps more and more these days; and more and more often, I go to her to sleep by her side. Hoping it helps. Hoping it keeps her from something.

I spend a long time trying to come up with words to comfort her, but it isn't words she needs; what she lacks is another mortal, a friend, someone to hold her tight in arms of flesh and blood. Someone who wants to tickle her, push her over onto the bed and gently kiss her eyelids, or her neck, someone to cradle and rock her. That's who she needs, but where to find him?

;

I encounter my father standing on a podium, delivering a speech to an immeasurable crowd of people. I'm dropped into his drawling voice, in the middle of a sentence, with nothing to go by, not a single point of reference, but after just two words I know he's reading his poem "A New Love Song to Stalingrad."

Amplified by hundreds of speakers that could have made the Andes out of a molehill, his words about Stalingrad ring out and descend like manna from heaven on the heads of the audience, who look up and beam, grateful for so much goodness, hands folded reverently, asking for even more. Stirred to the depths of their souls, cut to the bone by every syllable my father utters, their throats go dry, their eyes get moist. Everyone present feels a deep connection with everyone else, like children of the same father, who is now watching over them, singing.

The thought strikes me, fills me with pride: my father is a father to all of us! I am no longer alone, everyone on earth is my brother or sister.

One with the crowd, I do as they do. Cradled by the sweet sounds of his voice, his ceaselessly speaking voice like a mother's song I can drown in, I sink down and let myself go, completely and utterly detached from earth, people, life, fully accepting this state of detachment as the one his poems inhabit, they too broken free of the earthly reality they represent while being no less real, like fleeting moments, momentarily anchored impermanences, and I haul myself up by his sounds, hang them like a hammock and lie down, rock rock back and forth, deeply happy, like a baby and almost numb with calm, no longer hearing their meaning, until his next sentences suddenly bring me back with a start:

Those who in Holland spattered tulips
and water with bloody mud
and spread the scourge and the sword
now sleep in Stalingrad.

The words take me straight back to my mother. She is in The Hague, in Nazi-occupied Holland, where my father has left her, spattered with the same bloody mud, it seems to me now; left behind to rot in this swampy, bitter place – for not only does he not make use any of the possibilities open to him as a consul to get her out of the country (yes, there would even have been regulations and agreements about exchanges and the repatriation of family members of Chilean diplomats), he actively prevents their being put into force. She was taken to Westerbork.

Gone is my sunny hammock as I drift away from my father's voice on an ice-cold stream, cold as Siberia, icy like Stalingrad itself; shut out from the crowd I momentarily felt part of. If I surrendered myself to his words, I paid for it immediately, for they were the wrong words. He who condemned the occupation of Holland in the strongest words took every possible action to prevent the escape of his own wife, or rather ex-wife, shortly after losing their daughter, from the same Nazi-occupied region. My father goes on and on pontificating, but I leave the crowd, feeling an urge to hurl thunder and lightning at them though I soon recover myself.

;

I find my mother sitting on the edge of her bed. It's not an unfamiliar sight to me; she sits like this for days on end sometimes, hands in her lap, eyes fixed gloomily on a spot beneath the windowsill without actually seeing it. Darkness fills the room, even though it is morning and the spring sunshine floods in through the window. There is a small bay window with a table in it. It would be a perfect writing table and my mother regrets that she doesn't write.

Exactly the same houses stand – too close – on the other side of the street. Their color like the inside of seashells, a pearly white like the tiles of my grave, but there are no tiles, no luster, just the dry, dull, white plastered facades. Walls, and behind them, unknown others. Sometimes a living wayang puppet appears in a window.

She thinks out loud, muttering to herself, then continues her brooding in silence. Abruptly, she stands up from the bed and resumes her lament in a loud voice, pacing heavily up and down. I follow her with my eyes, until she just as suddenly switches back to a low, almost beseeching murmur. I've heard the words countless times in exactly the same order in the years since I died, and repeat them in my own head in the same plaintive tone of voice. I'm not doing this to make fun of her, I would never make fun of her, I think, the thought itself also a repetition of words I have phrased this way countless times in recent years (or were they weeks, months? By and by, time has begun to pass me by), but when my mother sits down on the bed again and interrupts my inaudible singing, I stop immediately and listen to her, patiently, devotedly, like a proper daughter. I notice it is the same monologue she directed at the hat peg the day before. Seeing her hat hanging on the wall reminds her of all the times she used to take it off the peg to visit her daughter in Gouda. Her hand reaching out to take it, the hand that belonged to her when her daughter was still alive, etched itself into her memory, and my long stay with my foster family now seems condensed into that single image.

Another day, sitting down on a stool triggers similar thoughts. The stool, stained dark green, resembles one that stood in the kitchen in Java; the chair Cooky used to sit on while grinding spices.

The image and the memories it evokes weave together into a screen of barbed wire, wood grain and dark red hat plush, and finally, slowly, merge and shift into one long, inextricable death wish.

Each time, my mother spins her cocoon tighter around herself, weaving herself into the room I keep returning to, pupating into a continuously muttering recluse. After a while I'm able to tell from just a stray shred of thought which line of reasoning she is following, which path she is taking down the dead-end street of desperation, just as I need only four words of my father's to recognize the poem he's working on at any given moment.

She addresses the last part of her monologue to the spot beneath the window, where a dark stain on the wall keeps attracting her eyes. Looking straight through it, she gazes into a dream world of the past, gets lost in it. She is no less a ghost than I am; a figure in a magic lantern, a wayang puppet of her own memory.

TWENTY-EIGHT

I HAVE TO GET OUT of the stifling room above the photographer's shop for a moment, and arrive just in time to attend the banquet the Mexicans are holding in my father's honor. The copious banquet, graced with the presence of two thousand friends, washes over the public life of Mexico City like a flood. My father is seated at the head of one of the tables like a king, allowing one of his eager subjects to top up his glass. They bow and scrape. It's fun to watch. From my point of view, they all look just like cut out newspaper dolls throwing shadows on the backdrop of the vast and empty Mexican sky, and it's as if my father is wielding the scissors, for he needs only cast a glance or extend a finger – not even so much as point at something – for the entire entourage to leap to their feet around him. I watch the scene for a while before mustering the courage to go closer.

My heart is pounding – a phantom heartbeat; and always that same strange mixture of relief and disappointment upon finding that I am invisible to those around me. I sit on the edge of the table somewhere, close to the back of my father's chair.

"Look! The princess!" I hear the marshal whisper to the lady-in-waiting, "Malva Marina has joined us – and what would Her Majesty like for breakfast this morning?"

"The usual, bacon and eggs!" I shriek. Carefully, I clamber onto the tabletop, making sure not to knock over any teacups or plunge my toe in the middle of a tortilla, and I dance to my father's court, cagey and cumbersome, I play the fool to the crowd of two thousand people seated at the long tables. Leaping gracefully from table to table, I let my white dress billow in the wind (look, Daniel's father, isn't it pretty!), even sit on the lap of a handsome young man, until I'm tired of my game. I spend a long time studying my father's face, his prematurely balding skull, his remarkable chubbiness. His hand reaching out for the food, his hand bringing food to his mouth. His mouth always in motion. When he laughs, small bits of egg are sprayed around, and he slurps his drink. The moment his mouth has finished eating, it reverts to talking. Then my father taps his glass, hastily wipes his greasy lips with his crumpled napkin, lets it drop down as he stretches his legs, fixes as many faces as possible with a determined, lingering look, waits until everyone is hanging on the words he has yet to utter, the words that are keeping his audience in suspense until he finally opens his mouth and out they come, forming a speech.

"Ladies and gentlemen," I hear my father say. "It has been a long time coming, but the moment is here at last. None of you know why you are at this banquet. You think you came here today to bid me farewell on my departure from your beautiful Mexico," (he follows this with several more words about Mexico), "but actually, I've led you up the garden path. I wanted to catch you off guard when I introduced you to the most important person in my life, someone I've kept hidden for many years so as not to spoil the surprise. Ladies and gentlemen, here she is – the girl you saw dancing on the tables just now: my beautiful daughter, Malva Marina."

Louder than ever, the applause swells up from all those hands, four thousand of them, and the clapping won't stop, is even accompanied by the banging of cutlery on the table and the furious stamping of feet, until my head swims, until I faint. By the time I come around, the banquet has ended. The bottles have been drained, the cleaning ladies are marching up and down clearing the tables. Two thousand forks, knives and spoons; seven hundred bottles emptied by the revelers, all vanish in the wings of the stage, the domain of the cleaning staff. My father, meanwhile, is strolling in the hills elsewhere, followed by a large crowd of his admirers. He marches on and they follow on his heels, slowing down when he pauses, picking up their pace when he suddenly forges ahead again with long strides, and I'm reminded of a *danse macabre* and of the Last Judgement, while he, the Messiah, describes to the resurrected the hills and countryside they are seeing with their own eyes at that very moment. His outstretched hand follows the rolling outlines. His audience hear fragmented sentences escape his lips, ask him to recite the poems they originated from. He rocks his head from side to side. He always rocks his head more than he shakes it, an almost apologetic denial.

Then he stops dead in his tracks with dramatic abruptness and says, "Unfortunately, I don't know any of my poems by heart. I've written so many, you must know, that if I tried to weave the various strings of water together they would flow into each other like a latticework of rivers and all turn into a clattering waterfall you couldn't make head or tail of." Pleased with this explanation, he folds his hands behind his back and, still standing, gazes out at the countryside, not deeming his admirers worthy of another word (the last sentence turning out to be his final one); his eyes follow the verdant curves, the fresh foliage in the valley below. He squints at the familiar birds, then to his amazement notices a condor, and turning to see if his admirers are still there finds that, alas, they've already disappeared.

Time to head back. Delia is looking for him. He can make her out in the distance, weaving through the crowd as if looking for something. He waves, and eventually she spots him. She walks toward him (as if having found what she had lost) and he walks toward her. The strides of two people moving toward the beloved other. The feet that have arrived before they arrive themselves. His arms, a few steps away from her now, stretched out toward her as far as they would go. Her face: a laughing moon. His face: a crying sun. Her arms also outstretched to

(and before I can finish this sentence, Delia and my father are already locked in a fervent embrace. He seemingly trying to crush her, she completely enveloped by him. His arms squeeze her to his burly body while she is beaming, scorched by perfect bliss, and I slink off).

TWENTY-NINE

I FOLLOW MY MOTHER'S GAZE out of the window and see the entire infrastructure of the country in which I died. Every cogwheel in its place. The empty, indifferent sky above it galls me. Silent and completely motionless, I am suspended above the earth like a condor; I would like to take all outcasts under my invisibly spread wings, but they stretch only into nothingness. I see the fenced-off farmlands, their crops combed in different directions, the roads like greyish riverbeds, the slow dots on wheels; and the shreds of clouds that are drifting between me and the world in which I died, occasionally hiding it from my view. Below me flows the network of the over-zealous railways that made the expulsion so easy. The freight trains moving along the tracks are packed with children, women and men that are being deported to extermination camps in Poland.

At the moment I draw my last breath on Wednesday, March 2, 1943, I can see the first of nineteen trains traveling to Sobibor from the Dutch transit camp Westerbork between that day and the 20th of July 1943.

Sobibor. As a child, you used to read words backwards, and to you, Robibos sounded like an amalgamation of Ronja the Robber's Daughter and the bow she carried on the cover of your book. Sobibor was actually a camp in eastern Poland, on the Chełm-Włodawa railway line. Your grandfather's parents, the grandparents of your father, were deported there. They died a few months after I did.

Szymborska was still in the land of the living at the time, in the very country where, after a three-day journey, the freight trains with Jews arrived from the Netherlands. And though she was holding down a part-time job as a railway official, she knew nothing of what was going on yet. In her memory of the war there are no Jews. Her memory only recorded their names:

> Across the country's plains
> sealed boxcars are carrying names:
> how long will they travel, how far,
> will they ever leave the boxcar –
> don't ask, I can't say, I don't know.

> The name Nathan beats the wall with his fist,
> the name Isaac sings a mad hymn,
> the name Aaron is dying of thirst,
> the name Sarah begs water for him.

> [...]

> That's-a-fact. The rail and the wheels.
> That's-a-fact. A forest, no fields.
> That's-a-fact. And their silence once more,
> that's-a-fact, drums on my silent door.

Silence, perhaps the silence of your grandfather. For what could he say? How could he have said it? Those names, then the silence. Was it the self-imposed silence of Theodor Adorno, of no poetry after Auschwitz? Was it an embarrassed silence, like that of Günter Grass – usually not shy when it came to drum-banging and trumpet-blowing – out of shame about his membership in the Waffen SS? No, Wisława Szymborska's silence was of a different kind, different even from the dumbstruck, cannot-begin-to-imagine-silence; it was simply the silence of complete and utter not-knowing, the silence that fell over all those names, whose bearers suddenly went missing while their lives, too, were slowly blanketed by the dust settling on them. A silence covered with the dust of Auschwitz, Sobibor, drawn over the rest of their lives.

The contrast to the large Jewish family and its teasing and ranting, its music and song, couldn't have been greater. The move from the hovel in the Jewish ghetto brought three whole rooms, a house full of light and air and the hope of an even better life. There was singing in the AJC, the Laborer's Youth Centre in The Netherlands, too: the song of the Red Falcons, about a world that is bright and free, tra la la la la, Red Falcons want to live in a world that is bright and free, tra la la la la – only the silence is left now. Shall I tell you, Granny Szymborska – you won't mind me calling you that – the story of Nathan, who was deported to Auschwitz but survived because he played the trombone so beautifully? His daughter, Hagar's aunt Marja, wrote a whole book about him.

Shall I tell you about Isaac, not the mad-hymn-singing name who went insane, that was Louis, whose parents had given him this modern name instead of Levi so he would fit in with the modern world of railway lines (oh, the bitter irony!), cinemas and electricity – but then, who would not go insane under such... it's actually hard to believe he was the only one of his family to... (the pen falters here). He started praying like one possessed. First they put him in the psychiatric ward of an Amsterdam hospital, from where he was taken to the Appeldoornse Bosch mental institution and finally deported to Poland.

Alida cried out for her son. There was also an Aaron, by the way, but he lived two generations later; generations who, thank God, though not due to Louis's compulsive praying, managed to survive.

And Isaac, as a Jewish baker, was given a *Sperre*, a respite *bis auf weiteres*, but even he. Together with his wife Schoontje. Their bakery was called "Vuysje Luxury Bakery," their name spelled with an extra-posh y instead of the Dutch ij. One of their last pictures in the family album, before life goes on without them, shows him pushing his bread delivery cart with the words "Vuysje Luxury Bakery" painted on it.

Shall I tell you, Wisława, about some of those hidden behind the names in the trains to Poland, the family of Hagar's father?

THIRTY

Before the wig and the dress coat
there were rivers, arterial rivers:
there were cordilleras, jagged waves where
the condor and the snow seemed immutable:
there was dampness and dense growth, the thunder
as yet unnamed, the planetary pampas.

Oh, Oskar, must you disrupt my father's stanzas with your drumming! I know you're trying to capture the cadence of rapture and revel in the vast pampas of my father's writings just like me, but please stop making that noise, it's giving me a headache! I'm talking endless plains, not migraines.

Man was dust, earthen vase, an eyelid
of tremulous loam, the shape of clay –
he was Carib jub, Chibcha stone,

Oskar, career midget, don't get off your miniature donkey, spur it to a trot, let's hurry to catch up with past times. I can see my father standing there, proud and tall. It is 1971, the year of the Nobel Prize, the hour of rich guttural sounds resonating at the Poetry International Festival in Rotterdam, of nasal announcements made by men in corduroy; it is the time of struggle and solidarity, Oskar, but please keep your drumming to yourself now!

> imperial cup of Araucanian silica.
> Tender and bloody was he, but on the grip
> of his weapon of moist flint,
> the initials of the earth were
> written.

And my father could read them! He only transcribed them, the initials of the earth, he deciphered the hieroglyphs of minerals, the runes of rocks, he could read the faces of people. Oskar, be quiet!

> No one could
> remember them afterward: the wind
> forgot them, the language of water
> was buried, the keys were lost
> or flooded with silence or blood.

But it didn't happen to us! We didn't go under in the silence. We drowned it out by shouting down our concealment. So all right, you can beat on your drum now, Oskar. Thump their ears like a boxer!

;

But all of a sudden, Oskarchen is digging his heels in. Glumly contemplating his drumsticks, one in each little fist, he tells me they were only given to him so he would drown out his father's shame. And before Daniel can stop him, Oskar snaps each drumstick over his knee, throws them on the ground and starts trampling on them, bawling.

"I was only brought to life to deflect attention from my father's

Waffen SS membership! All my drumming was meant to make my father look better than he was, not to make people sit up and listen." His face has turned scarlet; I've never seen him like this before. Lucia tries to comfort him. She crouches down beside him on the grass and puts her arms around him, which he grudgingly allows, then tries to pull him onto her lap, tenderly muttering into his ear that his father was very young at the time and that he later spoke out strongly and unequivocally against it.

"But the Waffen SS were the worst of all," Oskar screams back suddenly, tearing himself free from her embrace and going back to trampling the broken sticks deeper into the grass.

Daniel makes the next attempt. In as decisive a voice as he can muster, he says that Germany would not have been able to stomach the truth if Günter had told it earlier; that he timed the revelation deliberately to give the Germans the chance to process it. Surely, Oskar understands that. But he still insists he was betrayed. All that time, he says, he was drumming for the wrong reasons. He doesn't personally care what all of Germany thinks, but he, as a son, feels betrayed and ridiculed by his father. "Made a midget for nothing."

THIRTY-ONE

DURING HER DEPORTATION to Sobibor, the mother of your grandfather tortures herself with the question whether her son Nathan, your great-uncle, is acting wisely by letting his two – very young – children hide out in a stranger's house.

A day before my death on March 2, 1943, your great-uncle Nathan happened to step out of the family bakery in Amsterdam just in time to see all the patients and staff of the *Joodse Invalide* across the street being deported. Uncle Nonie, as you called him, witnessed the heavy-handed evacuation of the Jewish nursing home with his own eyes. Even the blind and the lame were manhandled outside along with everyone else, severely disabled people who were told they would be taken to Germany as laborers.

From that moment, he was firmly resolved to send his children into hiding. He had no idea whether or not the rumors of Jews being murdered were true, but wanted to be on the safe side for his children's sake.

His mother doesn't understand, calls him a bad father for housing Jeanette and Wim, four years and three months old respectively, with strangers far away from home. She believes that parents, particularly those of very small children, should stay with them under any circumstances.

Your grandfather is twenty-nine and about to become a father for the first time. He has to live on after losing both his parents, his sister with her husband and two young children, his favorite brother and most of his friends in the space of a couple of months. Only by not talking about the war can he bear to go on living.

A second child is born after the war: your father. He grows up to become a sociologist – he wants to understand war and oppression, and hopes this will help him contribute to preventing their repetition. But whenever he asks your grandfather about the war, the latter is silent. After reading your father's article about the people living in the vicinity of the Westerbork transit camp, he only comments, "Very interesting." You think that, in the face of all this silence, your father cast himself as the diligent boy writing everything down, trying to make sense of it all. But he himself is equally unable to talk about sensitive topics.

Your father leaves for Chile to witness a socialist experiment being conducted by a democratically elected socialist president: Salvador Allende.

When you are born, your father, who wants to go on traveling and writing, doesn't tell his parents or other family members, his colleagues or his friends for eleven years.

;

I've been looking over my shoulder all this time to see if I can spot your father anywhere. There he stands, conspicuously tall; head and shoulders above the Chileans surrounding him, he's wearing a burgundy jacket with eye-catching embroidery on the shoulders.

Your father is an outsider. My father, on the other hand, was something of a professional Chilean; he had an intuitive knowledge of everything going on in the hearts and minds of the Chilean people and expressed it in his *Canto General*, which was meant to be valid for all of Latin America.

Your father, coming from a socialist family, does not speak in hymns but in newspaper copy; he wants to discover the mechanisms of power and oppression, understand the underlying strategies and report on what he sees as impartially as is possible for an outsider. His own family history under the Nazis has provided him with an awareness of the dangers and an empathy with its victims.

It is the reason he returned to Chile in 1973; to give an account of the violence and suppression descending on the country that had become so dear to him.

THIRTY-TWO

AND THEN COMES THE DAY I see my father out. I find him lying dead on his hospital bed, grab the hand he used almost his entire life for writing, and together we drift over the rooftops of Santiago for a while. Far beneath us lie the presidential palace, the park, the stadium, the slums full of politicized workers and the Mapocho River. And there in the depth below him, my father sees the shuffling funeral procession accompanying him to his granite resting place flow through the streets like a living human branch of the river, while countless corpses are drifting down the Mapocho itself.

Your father is down there somewhere in that swelling crowd too, among the living. He has flipped open his writing pad and lets his pen glide over the paper while taking care not to be singled out by one of the carabineros that are watching like hawks. There he is, shuffling along with the crying men, women and children in my father's funeral procession. He observes everything and everyone, his face is tense, he turns his head all the time, recognizing the danger. Despite the obvious differences, your father's experiences in Chile remind him strongly of what he knows of the German occupation of the Netherlands: the curfew, the shots ringing out in the dark outside, the arrests, the corpses littering public places, the fear of betrayal by neighbors and acquaintances, the murders and the executions by firing squad.

Later, when the two of you have been reunited – o happy pair –

you'll watch the television footage together that you dug up from the station's archives, and when he appears on the screen, you'll be struck by how engaged he looks. He sees everything.

They arrive at the tomb. My father's coffin disappears inside, but instead of leaving, the crowd starts to sing. "Incredibly courageous people," your father notes, describing in his diary how the laments turn into protest songs against the junta while the carabineros' guns are aimed at the procession. The presence of so many journalists, who came to the country to report on Pinochet's coup, gives them the courage to speak out. They know that everything that happens there today goes on record, that there are cameras pointed at them as well as guns. My father's funeral becomes the first demonstration against the coup, two weeks after it took place.

;

We hear the battle cries, the internationale, the yell of the Communist Youth, and then:

"Pablo Neruda! Present! Now and forever!"

Beside me, my father starts humming, and I recognize his lines about the Mapocho River:

Mapocho River, when night falls
and, like a black recumbent statue,
sleeps under your bridges with a black cluster
of heads smitten by cold and hunger
like two immense eagles, O river,
O harsh river born of the snow

The black cluster of heads have yet again been smitten by hunger and cold in Chile, and my father, looking down now, can see that they have been joined in the river by the heads bitten off by a third eagle: the military junta. The wind seems to have a stronger hold on my father than on me, he's rising faster than I am. An icy blast, whim of his fever dream, is dragging him along with it, so I let him go; staring after him for a while until he has disappeared from view, still humming his wistful tune.

;

Oskar is banging his drum so loudly I think my eardrums are about to burst.

"Stop it, Oskar!" I scream, but he screams back that I had better watch out; the glass is shattering in the windows, objects wobble and fall over. I wake up in my father's house on Márquez de la Plata Street in Santiago.

I have often gazed at the beautiful earthenware, the black figurines and the white ones with the swans; and at the paintings my father and Matilde collected on their travels, each trying to mark out its own territory by outshining the others with its loud colors.

The house and all its contents, all its abundance and magnificent glory, has been reduced to rubble. My father himself, brought over from the hospital after his death, is lying on a bier among the debris, and three women, including his widow, are keeping a constant vigil at his coffin. Then, just as they are looking the other way at members of the junta entering the house to offer their feigned condolences on my father's death, I see the pen, which had slipped from his hand in the Santa Maria Hospital earlier, fall to the floor under the coffin.

La Patoja starts at the sight of the men standing among the rubble in their gaudy uniforms. The medals and decorations glint like shards of glass picked up from the floor and pinned to their chests. She scrutinizes their military outfits before turning her gaze to the endearingly humble checked shirt and jacket she dressed my father in to give him a more cheerful appearance, and the memories of the moments he used to wear this favorite attire of his bring a small, furtive smile to her face.

At that moment, I feel a first pang of sympathy for the woman who shared the last two decades of my father's life, and whom he told, just before dying, "It was beautiful to live, when you lived."

Those words had stung me with the bitter venom of jealousy at the time, but now that my father has been taken away from her too, all I can feel for this woman is pity. She can't help it that she loved him. Her eyes travel away from the checked collar again as she gazes tenderly into my father's face and the semi-ironic, last smile that seems fixed to it, as if laughing at everything present: death, the junta in their ridiculous military get-up, the slaughter going on outside the house to which he, having undergone it, will be immune in the future.

It is the afternoon of September 25, 1973. My father died two days earlier, the very day your father arrived in Chile. La Patoja's head is awash with a stream of memories of their good life together, and she reaches for a handkerchief to halt the progress of a tear that has just begun its meandering path down her cheek.

Memories are all that is left to you too now, and as I'm thinking this I quickly grab his fountain pen, as if the pen had a soul I now claim for myself – simply by taking possession of the thing, purely and simply because I believe that I, as his only offspring, have a right to it, and I use it to write this poem for my father:

It's

",   "
;· ·;··;

.   . " ".
·;··,,,,·,,, ,, ;··,,·

;··;

",   "
;· ·;··;

.   . "
·;··,,,,·,,

..   ".
;,,,, ;··,,·

.

;··;

. ....·
· ;,,,·

...

",   "
;· ·;··;

.   . " ".
·;··,,,,·,,, ,, ;··,,·

;··;

....
·;···,,,,,·,,·,,,,,,,,,,,··

..

....·
;·,,,·······

,,·

.
· ;··;

",   "
;· ·;··;

.   . "
·;··,,,,·,,

..   ".
;,,,, ;··,,·

raining the rain of Temuco.

I'm startled by one of the junta members approaching my father's coffin. His hard, ruthless eyes sweeping the room seem able to fathom everything, to see through it all, whether physically present or not, and I am starting to worry that he has even noticed me, however safely I'm dwelling in the inviolable state of being deceased, however invisible I think I am, and the man raises one eyebrow, stares at the place I am in for an unnervingly long time, finally scans my father's dead face before nodding almost imperceptibly as a sign of deference or goodbye and goes out of the room, leaving me in uncertainty whether or not he noticed me. Then the hubbub around me keeps getting louder. More and more people are streaming into my father's demolished house to ascertain for themselves his death with their own eyes, but there is no furniture, no couch or chairs; the looters have taken everything. A couple of friends go around to the neighbors' to borrow chairs, so those watching over the body of the deceased can do so sitting down. Furniture is dragged in, soup dished out, and the room soon becomes so busy and crowded I decide to retire to the upper floor, where nothing has been left intact either. Upstairs, in the bedroom, among the shards of window glass strewn all over the floor, I eventually find a spot where I can continue my writing, but even here I can't work undisturbed.

The place is crawling with journalists jostling to catch a glimpse of my dead father and the torched house.

La Patoja has ordered everything to be left precisely the way she found it on her return with my father's corpse. A smart move – now, all the world will be able to see what the junta has done to the house. Your father is one of the journalists who are there by accident because of the coup, and I read some of his notes in passing.

Neruda: went to pn first thing. On the wall opp. the house: pn, the Chilean youth salutes you. Inside the house (beautiful building) he is lying on a bier. Place barely tidied up after a fire (according to neighbors) or – more likely – a house search (according to protesters; not such a clear division between art/politics after all!) lots of broken glass.

In the middle of the swarming press, the body is carried out. The press being here is of course something of a coincidence.

The funeral procession: swelling somewhat; through working-class districts. Slogan: pn word!, present (three times) – now – and forever. One man keeps starting to recite a poem. Things get dramatic when we pass army barracks. The guards at the door do nothing – not even when the crowd, in reckless desperation, go on chanting the slogan as they walk past. What courage. There are only a couple of hundred people. By the time we approach the graveyard, the hearse is flanked by a ragged crowd of workers staring straight ahead. Almost 2000 people are waiting at the graveyard. A hundred meters before the entrance, I notice a jeep full of soldiers driving alongside.

Approaching the graveyard, there's a kind of roundabout; the procession goes around the right side, the soldiers (3 jeeps) take up position on the left. In the last few hundred meters, the crowd start singing the internationale – tentatively at first, by the end of the 2nd verse at full blast. At least half of the protesters are almost in tears as they enter the graveyard – not for pn, but for the president, and the failed reform. At the end of the ceremony, this is illustrated poignantly by the shouted slogan: *writer, president, one fighter!* Under the arch at the graveyard gate, last year's slogans are chanted for the first time: writer is exchanged for president; slogan of the left-wing youth. While members of the press are stepping, scrambling & crawling over the graves, the procession arrives at the tomb where a series of poets recite lengthy odes, whose appalling grandiloquence and longwindedness are a stark contrast to the artistry of the deceased. Only one boy, the last speaker for the left-wing youth, mentions not just nature, but also the humble, the poor he wrote about. pn came from Temuco – whose original inhabitants are now, according to Judith, being slaughtered and thrown into the river with impunity by the large landowners (who've been waiting for this moment). Slum dwellers sobbing by the tomb. The first demonstration. The internationale is sung a couple more times. Including when the coffin is taken into the tomb.

Afterwards: we are leaving the graveyard (the jeeps are still there) when we notice a crowd of people gathering at the door of the hospital beside the graveyard. Lists of the dead are nailed to the door. Names, identified and otherwise. – Behind each one it says whether they were a soldier or civilian. The ratio is about 1 : 10, as the whitecoat later confirms. When we go up to take a look we are accosted from all sides. A woman who lost her three brothers, crying. They weren't even involved with politics. Another woman, whose husband had suddenly disappeared. A couple of days later, she received a note saying her companion had been buried. Sobbing, she holds up his identity card. Another woman with her son is holding up a photograph of her other son, crying – got the same note. The wailing is coming at us from all sides now. Usually, they say, no one would have dared speak up. Now, they do: is it because of the crowd at the pn funeral? All these people are clothed very plainly. You listen, Koen takes photographs, and you don't have a clue what else to do.

Is this an exceptional moment? No, it's been like this since the 11th, doctor says. Usually more crowded. We dare not go back out for fear of the soldiers.

Coffins are carried outside. A woman following 3 coffins. People stop us: we must write about what is happening. Koen is asked to take pictures of the contents of 2 coffins: 2 young men, shot through the head. Her husband and her son, the whitecoat says. The first coffin contains her father. None of the three had anything to do with politics.

They come during the day, but more often at night, a woman says. Shooting whoever they want. Many of the corpses brought here have been fished out of the river, the whitecoat says. Every day, several dozens of corpses still arrive at the hospital, he has no idea where from. He has never seen anything like it, doesn't know what kind of world he lives in anymore.

Were these people involved in politics? No. So why were they killed? No answer. Murdered? No answer.

I'm still talking to the whitecoat when a young man buttonholes me, telling me he came from southtown to look for his father, who was arrested. He's 52 years old, looks such and such. The doctor advises him to make inquiries at the stadium first. He's been there, nothing. The Min. of Defense, then.

Press conference: govt. statement: regrets the death of Pablo Neruda. The junta has ordered that the family be offered condolences. Recognitions are still forthcoming.

;

The house of my dead father, where la Patoja is holding her wake at his coffin, is filling up with colonels and generals who come to offer the widow their condolences on the terrible loss suffered by her, not to mention all of Chile, but la Patoja, walking away and climbing the stairs to escape the hypocritical sympathy, answers under her breath, like a mantra only I can hear, "No, gentlemen, I will not accept your condolences."

A moment later she comes into what used to be their bedroom and plops down on the edge of what is left of their mattress.

We're sitting there together now, she and I, even if she doesn't know it. She thinks she is alone with her thoughts of my father and I let her get on with her brooding while giving myself over to mine again, so it takes a while for me to notice the shoulders of the woman on the bed are beginning to shake more and more violently, but then her sobbing becomes so shrill with grief that I have no other choice but to reluctantly put down my pen and look up at her.

I tuck the pen back behind la Patoja's right ear. "You go and write some beautiful memoirs with it," I mumble sincerely. "I'll come and borrow it from you next time I need it, I'm sure you won't mind."

She moves her head up and down in a way that I interpret as an indulgent nod.

Actually, the motion of her head only indicates that she has capitulated to her sorrow. Matilde Urrutia is wailing as if she has only just become aware of the universality and irreversibility of her loss, of how deserted she will be for the rest of her life in my father's absence; just as deserted as the rest of Chile at that moment, and as lonely as my mother and I were when he was still living life to the fullest, skilfully playing the lovestruck lover to his second wife Delia and then to her, Matilde. My mother and I were used to great losses, but to Matilde Urrutia, every second from that moment on would form a stark contrast to all the years she had spent together with my father and which had been steeped to the core in their togetherness. Everything she thought, everything she saw, reminded her of him, made her wonder what he would have made of it. She couldn't even look at herself in the mirror without imagining him seeing her through her eyes. I can feel her complete devastation, her doubt whether she can hold her own in this world – this nightmare world, from which, at that moment in history, neither the living nor the dead are able to wake.

Wistfully, she remembers his voice, the words he would wake her with so tenderly on some mornings.

"Lazy Patoja, how much longer are you going to sleep?"

There is no question that my father loved his third wife more than his first, my mother. Perhaps more than his second one, too. Certainly more than me. This is the truth, this is how it happened and nothing can be done to change it now. No matter how long I go on living after death or how much I ponder and chew over the temporary life that was my lot, it will never alter the way things were. It is an almost unacceptable reality, one I will have to reconcile myself to in death, which is why I get you to write it down for me again and again, to drum it into me.

I will never win back the love of my father. The one chance I had for that, during our lives, has passed.

I crumple up the poem I just wrote and toss it among the debris and broken glass and all the other rubble that is left of my father's house. Like a rose to go on his grave, and in solidarity with it.

THIRTY-THREE

WHEN MY FATHER DIES, the many funerals he has witnessed and described pass before his mind's eye. He thinks back at the death of his swan, which used to rub its neck on his face – from one moment to the next, it was dead.

He also witnesses, for the first time, the death of his mother, weakened by labor, unable to recover from it, succumbing to tuberculosis. He stands at her sickbed, takes her hand, strokes her forehead. He, too, can now go back in time, see what happened in his earliest youth before he was aware of it. Death can be relived an infinite number of times in ever-changing versions and with different casts of people, and each time it will feel like a unique event. They are in Parral, his mother is dying. She is in pain. He is unspeakably moved by seeing her there, seeing his father sit beside her, still young, younger than he can remember him. It is a fleeting image, he is only there at the moment of her death, and in this past, he comforts his mother, and in this past, she opens her eyes and summons all her fading strength to smile at him, very faintly, to let him know she has seen him and that seeing him has helped.

He sees the deaths of his friends, first the natural deaths, then the unnatural ones. Like me, he is gripped by the need to know all, even the most unbearable details. He now knows that on the other side of death is a place of calm from where you are an observer existing in a state of all-pervading tranquillity, whose gaze – though it can do nothing but look – is capable, just by looking, by seeing, to console the living for that which is unacceptable to them.

My father was there when Lorca was murdered. The bullet inched forward as if in slow motion, everything slowed down, there was no sound, only the realization, the bullet, death, and himself. The body keeling over. My father saw it, he knew who did it, and afterwards was able to help his friend at the moment of his death by letting him know he wasn't dying alone, surrounded only by his enemies, his murderers. That someone was waiting to guide him through death. He watched them shout at his friend Víctor Jara in the stadium of Santiago forty years later, crush his hands, put his guitar around his neck and jeer, "Go ahead, play!" And when they shot him dead, my father heard the poem that Federico, murdered four decades earlier, had written in better times, when the guitar itself had been enough to break your heart:

> The weeping of the guitar
> begins.
> Useless
> to silence it.
> Impossible
> to silence it.

[...]

My father witnessed how Miguel Hernández, terminally ill and shivering with fever on a sack on the filthy floor of his cell, gave up the ghost, and Miguel Hernández, knowing he was there, was not lonely at the moment he left his body, because he sensed he was not alone and he realized that his life had mattered.

And when I died, my father was suddenly there too, after his own death, and so I must now rewrite my version of the death scene in the play of my life as I watch him standing by my bedside, deeply moved, seeing how beautiful I am, how sweet, and I can tell he finally admits to himself that he has always loved me for who I was and never rejected me for who I could not be. He stands there with no self-reproach, regret or ridicule – such emotions have become meaningless and would only get in the way of his love for me. I sense his presence, and sensing it I also realize he has finally acknowledged I am his daughter and he is my father, and that this is actually the most important thing of all – that the how and why, the everyday reality of my daughterhood and his fatherhood is canceled out by this simple truth. The indelible, indisputable, true fact made fact by truth itself, beyond doubt or denial.

When my mother dies in 1965, alone in the last of countless Hague lodgings and in so much pain, my father, in one of the versions he relived later – not that long ago, actually – is finally there.

He shot through her mind just as she left the realm of the living. It was a bitter thought, a stab of pain, a question mark. And now he's standing there looking straight at her as if to say, "You see? I didn't leave you alone after all, not for good. Do you see now that we have always been part of one another's lives, even if I didn't say so in as many words in my memoirs?" The differences that had been between them have become completely irrelevant in this instant, and it is a powerful moment because of its absolute uniqueness, because it is her last living moment; the snap of the fingers that precedes death. The dying and those watching over them are simply too much in awe of death to dwell on the things that can ruin a whole life, and which seem no more than a distant worry to them now. White noise that the dying can no longer hear.

In her poem "Photograph from September 11," Wisława Szymborska wrote that there were only two things she could do for those who leapt from the Twin Towers in New York on September 11, 2001. The two things were: describe their flight and not add a last line (so they would never reach the ground). In the same way, there are just two things I can do for my parents: describe their flight and add all these lines.

;

And lifting my head, I see you sitting at the table in front of me writing them down for me, and I ask, "So what's it like to have a father? You were not even handicapped, and yet you didn't know him as a child, either. You first encountered him in a train. Your mother pointed at the man reading a book in the seat opposite you and said, 'That man is reading a book your father wrote.' Overwhelmed by a sense of pride, you repeated, in a voice so loud the whole compartment would hear it, 'That man is reading a book my father wrote, isn't he, mom?'"

The man opposite didn't even raise his head. No one in the compartment reacted. The book had caused a stir in left-wing circles because its critique of would-be leftists came from the left.

The cover showed a moustachioed man rolling a cigarette. He was not your father, though you thought that he was; that you were seeing your father for the first time, at five years old. In your mind, his authorship grew out of all proportion. You were convinced that everyone knew him except you, that everyone read his books. And later, when he looked after you for an evening, he cut out paper dolls from newspapers and held them up against the light, making beautiful shadow figures on the wall. He tucked you in and kissed you good night. Your mother had told him it was important for children to see their father at least once, to give them an idea of who he was. "You are my father, aren't you?" you asked, to make sure.

Later, when you were eleven, you started writing him letters. They worked – he fell for them, he obeyed them: your father came back. Isn't that a miracle? Yes, it is a miracle! That's why you're doing it again now. You're doing it for me, too. You're luring my father back to me. Let this piece of writing be my letter of recommendation to him.

;

It was 1983. Your father had just returned from his last, fruitless visit to Chile: going through customs at Santiago airport, the number 6 had appeared on the screen when his passport was checked. At the time, Chile was rife with political murders.

The man behind the counter made a call. *"No entiendo, señor. Aparece un seis."*

The airport authorities took your father away to a small room, where he was interrogated extensively for hours. How much truth was there in the rumors of his connection to Orlando Letelier, the Chilean former minister who was killed in a car bomb in Washington in 1976 by Michael Townley, the man later also associated with the so-called doctor who supposedly gave my father a lethal injection? Correspondence about your father had been found in Letelier's luggage, according to information issued by the FBI itself. Your father had worked together with Letelier in the campaign against the proposed investment of the Dutch Stevin Group in 1976. The investment eventually fell through, to the anger of the junta. Letelier had acted as a contact, and this ultimately led to his assassination.

There were articles about it in the newspapers, your mother carefully cut them out and kept the clippings in the low living room sideboard you'd sometimes sneak a look into. Your father had traveled to Washington to report on the trial, in which he had originally been called as a witness, for the *Haagse Post* weekly. He had appealed to Letelier for a letter of recommendation after being denied a visa in an earlier attempt to travel to Cuba. Thanks to Letelier's intervention, he managed to secure permission. This resulted in the *Washington Post* and *El Mercurio* writing about your father, calling him a Cuban secret agent, a sympathizing journalist, a pal of Letelier's.

During his interrogation at the airport, your father overheard the officials discussing whether to take him to the headquarters of the DINA, Pinochet's secret police, for further questioning. Instead, they eventually decided to expel him from the country as quickly as possible; he was sent back to the Netherlands on the same plane he'd arrived in, and which had waited for him.

And then he became your father. And after that, you got to know him as the father he has been to you these past three decades.

;

If you asked me who I loved most, my father or my mother, I'd tell you that my opinion on the matter tends to be variable. As a newborn baby, I was simply mad about my father. His dear, large head, his deep, nasal, cooing voice, his wholeheartness and potbelliedness, and his powerful arms, all sent me into raptures. His head appearing like a blazing sun above my cradle, bending over me, was absolute reassurance; nothing but pleasure as far as the eye could see, earth for my feet and my hands.

When, on the other hand, my mother bent over my cradle to lift me out and hug me to her chest, it was her eyes, her large, glorious mouth and her full head of black hair that attracted me like magnets. Close to her I felt absolute love, absolute presence, and even the closest closeness was not close enough to me. I constantly longed for the company of one of them. I lived only in the looks they gave me. If they turned their faces away, I was only half alive, as in sleep, in the shadows. They woke me up every so often, popping up out of nowhere, their kisses awakening a me inside of myself.

Then came the things. Large, immovable objects that would sometimes push in. The bars of a cot. The fringe on a cradle. Curtains drawn open or shut. Balcony balustrades, clouds, sky, distant vistas, leaves on the trees, ice cream cones, flowers and their scents. The things were claiming their right to an existence alongside my parents' presence, and I learned to lose myself in the buzz of a bluebottle, in the swaying shadow of a palm tree. Later still, only the eyes, the large glorious mouth and abundance of black hair kept looming up with clockwork regularity – besides the things, which had swallowed up the blazing sun and had drowned out the sonorous, deep, dark voice, so that I never heard it again. From then on, my horizon became an imaginary line in the distance. A vague something I had always been aware of but never certain; something that was missing. Until the eyes, mouth and hair also disappeared, making only sporadic, intense reappearances, and the others became friendly but faraway faces that all looked the same and uttered noises I didn't understand. Human muzak. Sea soup.

;

I arrive just in time to attend the banquet the Mexicans are holding in my father's honor. The copious banquet, graced with the presence of two thousand friends, washes over the public life of Mexico City like a flood. My father is seated at the head of one of the tables like a king.

"Ladies and gentlemen," I hear my father say. "It has been a long time coming, but the moment is here at last. None of you know why you are at this banquet. You think you came here today to bid me farewell on my departure from your beautiful Mexico," (he follows this with several more words about Mexico), "but actually, I've led you up the garden path. I wanted to catch you off guard when I introduced you to the most important person in my life, someone I've kept hidden for many years so as not to spoil the surprise. Ladies and gentlemen, here she is – the girl you saw dancing on the tables just now: my beautiful daughter, Malva Marina."

TRANSLATIONS OF POEMS & QUOTES

PAGE 7

"Godsake That Father of Mine," Hagar Peeters, translated by Vivien D. Glass

FROM: *Koffers zeelucht*, Uitgeverij De Bezige Bij, 2003

PAGE 43

"Thomas Mann," Wisława Symborska, translated by Stanisław Barańczak and Clare Cavanagh

FROM: *Poems, New and Collected*, Harcourt, 1998

PAGES 89-91

"Unity in Her" and "Come Always, Come," Vicente Aleixandre, translated by Dr. Robert Mowry

FROM: *Destruction or Love: La Destrucción o el Amor*, Susquehanna University Press, 2001

PAGE 107

"Song for the Mothers of Slain Militiamen," Pablo Neruda, translated by Richard Schaaf

FROM: *The Poetry of Pablo Neruda*, Farrar, Straus and Giroux, 2003

PAGE 139

QUOTE FROM: *Pablo Neruda, Memoirs*, translated by Hardie St. Martin, Farrar, Straus and Giroux, 1977

PAGES 142-145

"Verses on the Birth of Malva Marina Neruda," Federico García Lorca, translated by Keith Payne

PAGE 144

"How much does a man live, after all?," Pablo Neruda, translated by Magda Bogin

FROM: *The House of the Spirits* by Isabel Allende (epigraph),
Alfred A. Knopf Inc., 1985

PAGES 154-155

"Tarsier," Wisława Symborska, translated by Stanisław Barańczak and
Clare Cavanagh

FROM: *Poems, New and Collected*, Harcourt, 1998

PAGES 156, 157

"Thomas Mann," Wisława Symborska, translated by Stanisław Barańczak and
Clare Cavanagh

FROM: *Poems, New and Collected*, Harcourt, 1998

PAGE 168

"A New Love Song to Stalingrad," Pablo Neruda, translated by Donald D. Walsh

FROM: *Residence on Earth (Residencia en la tierra)*, W.W. Norton & Co. Inc., 1973

PAGE 176

"Still," Wisława Symborska, translated by Stanisław Barańczak and Clare Cavanagh

FROM: *Poems, New and Collected*, Harcourt, 1998

PAGES 179-180

"Amor America," Pablo Neruda, translated by Jack Schmitt

FROM: *The Poetry of Pablo Neruda*, Farrar, Straus and Giroux, 2003

PAGE 186

"Winter Ode to the Mapocho River," Pablo Neruda, translated by Jack Schmitt

FROM: *Canto General*, University of California Press, 2011

PAGE 197

"The Guitar," Federico García Lorca, translated by Cola Franzen

FROM: *Selected Verse*, Farrar, Straus and Giroux, 2002

ACKNOWLEDGMENTS

First, I want to thank De Bezige Bij: without my publisher, this book would not exist, and certainly not in this form.

I would like to thank many people, including of course my father, who gave me generous access to his unpublished Latin American diaries (1968, 1970, 1972, 1973 and 1983) as well as complete freedom to quote from them, and who commented on my manuscript. "Koen," who appears in his notes is Koen Wessing (b./d. Amsterdam, January 26, 1942 – February 2, 2011), the well-known photographer who accompanied my father in Chile in 1973.

Many thanks also to Giny Klatser-Oedekerk (February 21, 1928 – June 25, 2018) for our conversation about Malva. Her discovery of Malva's grave in Gouda in 2004 was the event that first prompted me to write this book. I want to thank my aunt Marja Vuijsje for letting me quote a number of passages from her book *Ons kamp, een min of meer joodse geschiedenis* (Our Camp, a more or less Jewish story) almost verbatim, which was the best way of doing justice to my great-uncle Nathan's original memories. My thanks also to Antonio Reynaldos for his invaluable help in finding information, images and people, Fred Julsing for sharing his childhood memories of his foster sister Malva with me, as well as Bernando Reyes for giving me access to his family archives and his personal photo archive of Pablo Neruda. I want to thank the Fundación Pablo Neruda, and especially Darío Oses, for access to Neruda's correspondence. I am very grateful to Claudio and Susana Pérez for letting me finalize my novel in their beautiful house in Isla Negra. I thank Maria Barnas for allowing me to share in her childhood memories of Roald Dahl, and Maarten Steenmeijer for his useful comments on my manuscript.

I thank the Royal Tropical Institute for enabling me to conduct my research into the parents and ancestors of Maruca Reyes, alias Marie Hagenaar – up until the moment this archive was sadly closed down due to budgetary cuts. The archive allowed me to find articles about and by Maruca's father Richard Pieter Fedor Hagenaar (Batavia, May 14, 1856 – Weltevreden, March 5, 1920), published in various Dutch Indies newspapers from the end of the 1890s till the 1920s. I made grateful use of David Schidlowsky's pioneering research into the lives of Maruca, Malva Marina and Neruda, as well as Adam Feinstein's Neruda biography, and would like to thank them both for our conversations about Malva Marina at the memorial ceremony in 2005 in Gouda. I am also indebted to Dominic Moran for his biographical work on Neruda, to Ian Gibson for his work on Federico García Lorca and to Carol Loeb Shloss for her biography of Lucia Joyce, as well as to *The Daily Mail* and Suzanna Andrews at *Vanity Fair* for their articles on Daniel Miller. I consulted Anna Bikont, Joanna Szczęsna and Artur Sandauer's work on Wisława Szymborska and have gratefully drawn on Fernando Sáez's biographical work on Delia del Carril. I also made grateful use of Jean Gelman Taylor's research into the Van Riemsdijk family. I owe a great debt of gratitude to the International Writers Program in Iowa; my residency in 2009 proved very fruitful for this book, as did the conversations I had there with Roberto Ampuero about Neruda and Malva. I want to thank the library of the University of Iowa for allowing me to consult its extensive research collection on Neruda. My thanks also to Camp Westerbork Memorial Center and the Dutch Red Cross for access to Marie Hagenaar's file on her internment in the Westerbork transit camp. Also my grateful thanks to my American publisher Carrie Paterson and my English translator Vivien D. Glass. Finally, I want to thank Sabry Amroussi, Patrick Pubben, Rob Schouten and Sander Kok for their unflagging friendship, our many conversations and their comments on drafts of my manuscript.

The observant reader will notice echoes of the opening sentences of *In Patagonia*, by Bruce Chatwin, and of poems by Remco Campert, Paul van Ostaijen, Vasalis and Stevie Smith.

Any resemblances between Neruda and my father, Maruca and my mother, and Malva and myself are completely and mischievously deliberate.

Malva's afterlife nickname Malvie is entirely of my own invention.

Amsterdam, July 2018